PARANORMAL

Dangers & Empty Mangers

TRIXIE SILVERTALE

Sittin' On A Goldmine Productions L.L.C.

Sittin' On A Goldmine Productions, L.L.C.

info@sittinonagoldmine.co

www.sittinonagoldmine.co

ISBN: 978-1-952739-03-3

Cover Design © Sittin' On A Goldmine Productions, L.L.C.

Trixie Silvertale
Dangers and Empty Mangers: Paranormal Cozy Mystery : a
novel / by Trixie Silvertale — 1st ed.

[1. Paranormal Cozy Mystery — Fiction. 2. Cozy Mystery — Fiction. 3. Amateur Sleuths — Fiction. 4. Female Sleuth — Fiction. 5. Wit and Humor — Fiction.] 1. Title.

CHAPTER 1

I'M HAVING what some might call a unicorn moment. Now, that may sound magical and unique, but, honestly, it's just abnormal and a little irritating. The unicorn, on this day, is standing in a queue. I know it doesn't sound like much, but, trust me, it has never happened to me since my arrival in Pin Cherry Harbor.

Oh sure, back in Sedona, Arizona, I used to have to stand in lines for all sorts of reasons. I would find myself waiting in a line at the checkout lane in a grocery store while a hapless tourist prattled on about their amazing experience at the whatchamacallit vortex.

Or perhaps I'd wait in a queue to pay for my gas as an old-timey local counted out dimes from their leather satchel to pay for a lottery ticket.

And let's not forget the joy of standing in line at the post . . . Oh, wait! Now I'm just making things up. I've never seen the inside of a post office in my life!

Honestly, though, I've never had to wait in a line for anything since I rode inside a smelly bus for nearly two days to arrive in almost-Canada and claim my inheritance.

Which leads me to my reason for standing in this abnormal line. This morning my grandmother and I—and, to be clear, that would be the ghost of my grandmother, which is tethered to the bookshop she left me in her will—were having a discussion about how much my life has changed. I talked about how fantastic it's been getting to know the father I thought dead, and how much better it is to have money than be trapped in either a poorly run foster home, or a dead-end barista job.

The foster system wasn't all bad, but it was mostly bad. There were a few good families in the mix, though. Foster mom number four really taught me to embrace my differences and appreciate the legacy of tenacious independence my mother left when she was taken from me so tragically. It's hard to lose a mother at any age, but for an eleven-year-old only child, discovering you're an orphan feels like the world stops spinning and kicks you into outer space just for fun.

What was I talking about? Oh, right. Standing in line.

The morning's wardrobe-related discussion with Ghost-ma uncovered a piece of her precious couture she can't remember picking up from the dry cleaner before she died.

Her exact words were, "Mitzy! This is serious! That Vivienne Westwood Worlds End Black 'Witches' Trench Coat is like one of my children! You have to rush over to the cleaners this instant. No one is getting a wink of sleep until I know it's safe."

So here I am, standing in line at said cleaners. A line of three people, which I can assure you, is unheard of at this latitude.

Each time Tanya disappears into the back to retrieve items of clothing, she stirs the atmosphere and a fresh wave of chemically impregnated air wafts over me. Ew.

Finally reaching the front of the queue feels like winning a marathon. Or, rather, what I imagine it would feel like to win a marathon, as I've never run more than a block or two in my entire life.

"Good morning, Tanya. I'm looking for a very special Vivienne Westwood coat my grandmother thinks she left here." As soon as the words are out of my mouth, I realize my mistake. "I mean, her will mentioned she left here." Lame save, but at least I tried.

The woman peers over the top of her half-moon readers. "Isadora passed almost three years ago. You can't be serious?" Her straight grey locks barely move as she shakes her head and rolls her wide-set eyes.

My heart sinks. "It was really special to her. Can you check?" It's also worth a small fortune, but I don't want to mention that.

The proprietor returns pretty quickly, and shakes her head a second time. This one comes with a scoop of silent "I told you so."

"Thanks for checking." I smile, nod, and exit. Well, I better embellish the bejeezus out of that search when I tell Grams the story.

Outside Harbor Cleaners, the endless winter has our tiny town in its grip. Last night I had to snuggle my uncooperative caracal underneath two thick down comforters to keep from freezing to death.

Before I make the run to my Jeep, I tug my stocking hat down over my snow-white hair, turn up the collar of my puffy jacket, and shove my hands into thick woolen mittens.

Pushing open the door, I jog for the Jeep. I can't risk an out-and-out run, due to hidden patches of ice lurking beneath the poorly shoveled sidewalk. I'm not exactly what one would call *coordinated*.

Ecstatic that I've made it to the vehicle and still manage to reside on my feet, I yank open the door and hop inside.

It's not warmer; it's just not as windy. And windchill can be deadly.

Poking the key into the ignition results in a fat load of nothing. There's a strange whine and a click, but there's no vroom vroom.

Cars are not my thing.

My father is out of town with his new wife on an important business trip, securing much-needed donations for the Duncan Restorative Justice Foundation.

Hmmmm. Hopefully, this is one of those boyfriend-to-the-rescue scenarios. Shivering as I remove a glove and hit the speed dial for Sheriff Erick Harper, I opt for speaker and try to keep my teeth from chattering.

His deep voice warms me. "Hey, I was just about to text and see if you were interested in an early lunch at the diner."

"I'd give you my great minds speech, but I'm currently stranded outside the dry cleaners and my Jeep won't start."

Sheriff Too-Hot-To-Handle launches into action. "I'll be there in ninety seconds. Don't do anything foolish."

The call ends before I have a chance to express how rude it is for him to assume that I would do something foolish. However, my reputation precedes.

While I wait for my knight in shining polyester to navigate the three blocks from the sheriff's station, I engage in a silent argument with my stomach.

"The patisserie is right around the corner. I could dash over to Bless Choux and grab coffee and a chocolate croissant." My tummy growls with encouragement. "But I'd likely freeze to death and poor Erick would find nothing but a broken down vehicle and a frozen human statue of his former girlfriend." A sharp pain stabs in my gut.

Before the internal battle can continue, the local sheriff arrives Code 3. For you civilians, that means lights flashing and sirens blaring! Yeesh. I'm sure he was concerned for the safety of his citizens, but now I feel like a real putz. Luckily, I'm about to be severely distracted.

Tall, blond, and ruggedly handsome Sheriff Harper hops out of his cruiser, tugs at the flaps of his deerstalker hat, and eases open my driver's side door. "At your service, Miss Moon. Would you like to take care of the abandoned vehicle first or head straight to the diner?" His smirk indicates he already knows the answer.

"I would prefer to go directly to the diner. In fact, I'm strongly considering abandoning the vehicle permanently."

He offers me a hand and I step out of the Jeep, gripping his arm with the claws of death as he guides me back to his car.

Not for the first time, I'm pleased to be getting in the front seat of a police vehicle.

"You know there's a fine for abandoned vehicles, Moon. I recommend you call a tow truck and have your vehicle properly processed at the junkyard."

You guessed it, properly processed gives me the giggles. "Ever since my car got hot-wired, it's been giving me nothing but trouble. The headlights go dark for no reason, the radio cuts out every time I go over a bump, and the windshield wipers only have one speed—psycho fast. There's no way I'm taking that thing home. I'll call a tow truck."

He dips his head in that way that insinuates he's doffing a cap, and jogs around the front of the vehicle. Even in a heavy winter coat, that man can melt my heart.

"What were you doing at the cleaners? Actually, what were you doing out and about so *early* in the first place?"

"Hilarious. I do plenty of stuff before 10:00 a.m."

"I'm sure you do. But you do realize it's almost 11:30, right?"

I actually had no idea it was that late in the morning, but I'm not going to give him the satisfaction of finding out. "Of course. That's why I'm so ready for lunch."

He chuckles, and his big blue eyes sparkle. "Oh, that's why, is it?"

"Hilarious, Sheriff Smarty-Pants."

His soft kiss on my lips prevents any further debate.

Should I tell him about the coat? He's not into designer fashion and he definitely won't understand Ghost-ma's obsession with a single piece. Plus he might tease me about running errands for apparitions, and he already has enough ammo.

"Moon? Moon, where'd you go?"

Whoops! That would be me getting all wrapped up in my mind movies and forgetting about reality. "Nowhere special. Definitely nowhere as great as Myrtle's Diner."

My favorite local haunt is a quaint diner named after my grandmother. Her original name, that is. She goes by Isadora now, but when she was married to her first husband Odell Johnson, they opened the diner together.

I recently discovered that Odell Johnson is my father's biological dad and my actual grandfather. So despite the fact that I spent over six years in the foster system in Arizona, believing I was an orphan, my family continues to grow by leaps and bounds the longer I hang out in Pin Cherry Harbor.

Erick parks in front of the sheriff's station and escorts me into the diner.

Warmth and welcome envelop us as we stamp off our winter footwear on the doormat and slide into our favorite booth.

Waitress extraordinaire, Tally, greets us with two steaming mugs of java. Her flame-red hair twists into a tight topknot, as usual, and her ready smile makes us feel like family.

I glance toward the orders-up window and my grandpa offers us his standard spatula salute through the red-Formica-trimmed opening.

Sheriff Harper removes his coat and places it on the red-vinyl bench seat. "So what were you doing at Harbor Cleaners?"

"Oh, right." Pasting on a smile, I take a deep breath and hope for the best. "Grams suddenly re-membered a special couture coat she left there a few years ago."

Erick nods, walks his hand across the table, and turns his palm up. I slip my hand in his before I continue.

"Tanya was obviously annoyed with my 'years too late' request."

He smiles as he glides his thumb along the back of my hand. "Success?"

"Negatory, good buddy. The coat was long gone. Grams will be devastated. I'd say that I don't care, but she'll probably make me search the world for a replacement. Hooray. So, I care, but not about the coat." We share a chuckle at Myrtle Isadora's expense.

Odell Johnson approaches the table, and the luscious aromas of our breakfasts waft toward us. I love that he always knows what his customers want. It's nice to be somewhere that feels so comfortable.

He places my standard chorizo and scrambled eggs with a side of golden home fries in front of me, and Erick gets a lovely stack of blueberry pancakes.

I open my mouth to request—

Odell retrieves a bottle of Tabasco sauce from his back pocket and sets it down before I can even begin to ask.

"Thanks, Gramps. You're the best."

He runs a weathered hand through his utilitarian grey buzz cut and clears his throat to hide his emotions. "It may take me some time to get used to that."

"Don't worry, I'll say it as often as possible, Gramps. Maybe we can cut that time in half."

He chuckles and raps his knuckles twice on the silver-flecked Formica table.

Rather than returning to the grill, he grabs the local paper from the counter, heads back to our table, and tosses it in front of me. "I figured you'd get a kick out of the headline."

He saunters toward the kitchen with no further explanation.

I glance at the photo of the First Methodist Church's Nativity scene and notice a strange anomaly. That's when my eyes are drawn to the headline "Where is God?"

My mouth falls open and, as my mischievous grey eyes catch Erick's, we both point at the image of the empty manger beneath the clever header and laugh out loud.

"I'd have to say Quince Knudsen hasn't headed back to college yet. The patriarch of the Knudsen clan did not write that headline. Quince's father is far too verbose, and worried about his newspaper's reputation, to come up with a pithy header like that."

Erick nods in agreement. "It's such a minor theft, I hate to lose any manpower looking into it. Would you mind?"

For a moment, I feel like I'm in one of those movie scenes where the camera pulls back rapidly and the room around the main character shrinks into the distance. And, as a film school dropout, I know what I'm talking about. "Did I hear you correctly? Are you officially hiring me for a case?"

He grins and shoves a maple-syrup-dripping bite of blueberry pancakes into his mouth.

I wait impatiently while he politely chews before answering.

"Not official. It's more like a boyfriend asking a girlfriend for a favor."

"Oh, in that case, I'm definitely too busy."

His jaw drops and his eyes widen. "Seriously?"

"Gotcha. Of course I'll look into it. I would've looked into it whether or not you asked me. The photo alone is enough to get my attention. Quince has got skills."

CHAPTER 2

SINCE I'M DOING a girlfriend favor by looking into the missing baby Jesus from the First Methodist Church's manger, Erick is doing a boyfriend thing by taking care of my abandoned vehicle.

I have to get a new winter vehicle, though. I absolutely can't drive my grandmother's 1957 Mercedes 300SL on salted roads in blizzard conditions. In the meantime, I'm sure my dad won't mind if I borrow his truck while he's away.

Once I get my wheels sorted, my first stop is the office of the *Pin Cherry Harbor Post*. If, as I suspect, Quince Knudsen is still in town, he's my best lead. Not that he'll give up the information for free, but once I toss a little cabbage his way, the info should flow.

As soon as I enter the old brick building, which

houses the local paper, I can smell the ink. It always reminds me of my bookshop, but in a raw, straight-to-the-source kind of way. I approach the birch-clad reception area and walk straight past the bell, which squats below a sign instructing me to ring it.

I do not.

Instead, I head into the room behind the desk and find my quarry.

Quince twists from side to side in a dilapidated office chair as his fingers tap furiously on an ancient keyboard.

"Hey, when do you head back to Columbia?"

"Two weeks."

Welcome to Conversational Skills 101 with Quincy "Quince" Knudsen. This kid is a flipping genius with a 35mm camera, but he can't be bothered to put more than three words together in casual conversation.

"Got it. Did you take the empty manger pic?"

"Yah."

Keeping my chuckles to myself, I press on. "Who reported the crime?"

Shockingly, my question causes him to cease his assault on the keyboard and swivel toward me. He flicks his sandy-brown hair out of his eyes as he asks, "Crime?"

"Yeah. You don't think the baby Jesus got up and walked away on his own, do you?"

Quince snickers before he replies. "Not 'til Easter."

"Touché." I admire his quick wit. "Anyway, I figure someone took it as a prank. Sheriff Harper asked me to look into it. Who called it in?"

The young man shrugs. "No one."

And so begins the figurative pulling of the teeth. "All right. If no one called it in, then how did you know to stop by and get the picture for the front page?"

"It's on my way."

Taking what I've learned from past conversations with the photojournalist, and adding a soupçon of psychic skills, I deduce that the First Methodist Church lies along Quince's route to work. "Were you driving by on—?" It takes me a minute to remember what day of the week it is, how many editions of the *Post* there are per week, and when those editions would be put to bed. "You were driving to work on Tuesday and noticed the empty manger, and grabbed some photos. Right?"

"Yah."

I'm gonna go ahead and call that a success. "Do you know anyone at the church that I can talk to?"

"Nope."

"Copy that. Have you heard of any other holiday decorations going missing?"

"A couple plastic reindeer."

"Thanks. If I need more information on that, I'll let you know. And if you hear anything, or anyone reports an abandoned baby Jesus, you'll text me?"

"What's it worth?"

And there it is. My succinct source has a price. "How 'bout I drop a couple bills now, and a couple more if you come up with anything useful?"

He nods. "Sweet."

Sweet indeed. This guy sits in a chair, offers me a handful of words, and makes forty bucks. Must be nice. I grab two twenties from my pocket and hand them over.

Lucky for him, I've lived in the town that tech forgot long enough to learn that cash is king. Other than the credit card slidey machine I once observed with wonder at the dry cleaner, I've been living on a strict cash-only diet in almost-Canada.

As I turn to leave, there's a mumbled, "Thanks, dude," tossed in my wake.

At my bookstore, the search for the ghost of grandmothers past is underway. First stop, the third floor of the printing museum, past the photo-engraving exhibit, where Isadora enjoys working on her memoirs.

She recently received some positive feedback from a publisher who indicated they were interested in seeing the first several chapters. However, she's been dragging her ethereal feet and has yet to submit the requested materials. If you ask me, she enjoys writing and the *idea* of publishing a fair bit more than the rigors of literally publishing.

Third floor: no joy.

The trip back down the stairs to the first floor takes me through the large equipment exhibit and past our authentic Gutenberg press. I pause to admire the ancient machine before walking through the Employees Only door, back to the main floor of the bookshop.

Quietly making a serpentine path through the stacks, I confirm we are patron free before I start shouting. "Grams! Grams! Where are you?"

As predicted, my outburst does not produce the desired response. Instead of a ghost materializing at my beck and call, the heavy stomp of biker boots echoes off the tin-plated ceiling. Is it my imagination or is the enormous chandelier actually shaking a little? Kind of like the water in the glass in *Jurassic Park*?

While I puzzle over the physics of my query, my volunteer employee Twiggy stops in front of me, crosses her arms, and shakes her severe grey pixie cut in my general direction. "I hope you at least scanned for customers before you started hollering."

"I did."

She nods once, but then shakes her head. "I'd ask if you were trying to wake the dead, but I suppose you are." Twiggy cackles mercilessly at my predicament.

I'm happy to oblige. The woman works for free and seems to sustain herself solely on my haphazard personal misfortunes. Nothing serious mind you, just the occasional tumble onto my well-padded backside; or, before things got serious with Erick, there were some massive lovelorn mistakes. "I hate to ask, but have you seen any sign of Isadora or even Pyewacket?"

She tilts her head and nods slowly. "I fed his royal furriness this morning. He gobbled it up and ran to scratch at the back door. When I pushed it open, he took one look at the snow in the alley, twitched his black-tufted ears and hustled his tan backside up to the loft. Last I saw, he was snuggled up on the shelf next to your copy of *Mastering Artisan Cheesemaking*."

"Copy that. I'll check the apartment for Grams. Thanks."

I head for the wrought-iron circular staircase, but Twiggy doesn't budge. As I grip the curvy banister and attempt to climb over the "No Admittance" chain—which she insists be hooked up 24/7 —I teeter for a moment, catch myself, and land with a clamor on the other side.

She scoffs, clearly sorry I didn't cause a greater spectacle, and trudges into the back room.

At the top of the staircase, I take a moment to appreciate what I have. Scanning the beautifully curved mezzanine and its massive collection of arcane tomes, I breathe in the possibility of endless worlds. The oak reading desks are perfectly aligned, as usual, and each of the green-glass lampshades stands ready for action. Striding across the thick Persian rug, I pull down the sconce that serves as the candle handle, activating my sliding bookcase door.

No ghost pops out to greet me.

"Grams? Pyewacket? Is there anyone here who can help me with this case?"

Isadora morphs through the wall from the closet I call *Sex and the City* meets *Confessions of a Shopaholic*, and stares at my empty hands. "Where's the coat?"

"About that—"

She shimmers and the air in the room seems charged with electricity. "If Tanya thinks she can get away with selling a dead woman's—"

"Grams! Don't assume the worst. It's been several years. Tanya promised to ask her daughter-in-law if she remembered the coat. We're still working on it."

She fades and drifts aimlessly in my general direction.

"Hey, what's wrong? This can't all be about an old coat."

Her aura dims. "I was hoping to see Odell."

Oh boy, this is definitely my fault. Once I discovered Odell was my biological grandfather and pulled him into the small inner circle of people who know Isadora's ghost haunts my bookstore, I immediately became a matchmaker for afterlife romance.

"It's not like that, Mitzy. We grew close before I passed away."

Which brings me to my next point. "Grams, I'm sure you're as tired of hearing me say it as I am of having to say it, but you're not allowed to drop in and read my thoughts anytime you please."

She opens her translucent mouth to give her standard speech about how things are all muddled up, but I head her off at the pass. "If these lips aren't moving, you're not allowed to comment. That's our agreement, and I would really appreciate it if you would abide by it even thirty percent of the time."

Her standard "Well, I never" retort is not offered. She really is in a mood.

"I'm—"

"Grams!"

"Sorry." She twists one of her large diamond

rings and gazes out the six-by-six windows overlooking the harbor.

"Beg your pardon, but that word is supposed to mean something. 'Sorry' is hardly worth saying if you simply plan on breaking the rules again ten seconds later."

She hovers above the settee and grumbles under her breath.

"What was that? I didn't exactly hear what you said."

Ghost-ma groans and presses a bejeweled hand to her forehead. "I said, if you loved me as much as you say you do you'd fetch Odell."

I flop onto the scalloped-back chair and inhale sharply through my teeth. "I have a tiny problem with that. Maybe two. I'm not a dog, and Odell has a business to run. There are people in this town who depend on him for his amazing food and life-giving coffee."

My gentle teasing does the trick, and a hint of a smile graces Ghost-ma's lips.

"If it will make you feel better, I'll stop by later today and make sure he's planning a visit tonight."

Her glowing eyes gaze down at me with love. "And that's why you're my favorite granddaughter!"

"Thanks, but I'm your only granddaughter. Aren't I? Apparently, you've been holding out on me with a few hidden limbs of the family tree, so it doesn't hurt to double-check."

"Oh, Mitzy, you're such a card."

"I am indeed. Before you get sidetracked with your afterlife love life, I have some investigative questions."

She squares her designer-gown clad shoulders, smooths her burgundy silk-and-tulle Marchesa burial gown, and adjusts one of her many strands of pearls. "Ask away. I'm here to help."

"Thanks. I know you ran in a lot of different social circles and greased a lot of palms in this town, but I wasn't certain of your religious affiliations."

"They came and went. Why do you ask?"

"Did you happen to have any at the First Methodist Church?"

Her glow increases and her smile widens. "As a matter of fact, my fourth husband, Joe Willamet, was a devout Methodist. And he left a significant gift to the church when he passed. If I hadn't already been—"

"Three times divorced and rolling in cash?"

"Listen here, young lady, that nest egg I built is serving you quite nicely."

"You're not wrong." I offer her a grateful smile. "Back to my thing. I need some information regarding a missing baby Jesus. Whom should I talk to?"

Grams coughs, snorts, and nearly chokes in surprise. "Oh, sweetie. You really have to take this show on the road."

Taking a mock bow, I humor her. "I'll think about it. Any contacts?"

"The minister is very tightlipped and a tad standoffish, but the church secretary is an absolute sweetheart. Although, do not let her catch wind that you're dating the sheriff. She's a hopeless gossip!"

I slowly get to my feet and place a fist firmly on my hip. "And in this scenario, are you the pot or the kettle?"

Her laughter tinkles like soft bells as she vanishes through the bookcase into the bookstore beyond.

CHAPTER 3

THE FIRST METHODIST CHURCH is on a side of town that I don't have much reason to visit. So, when I pull into the parking lot, the unfamiliar sights momentarily flabbergast me.

Ambling across the snow-crusted asphalt, I take my time admiring the simple but impressive structure. The main sanctuary's massive arched roof supports a single black steel cross protruding from the peak with a flame shape swirling up on the left. The grand entrance is all glass, allowing a near-perfect view through to the elaborate stained-glass wall behind the pulpit.

The front doors are open, so I let myself in and meander down the center aisle, temporarily mesmerized by the floor-to-ceiling glass mosaic.

The image depicts Jesus cradling a lamb, and

the bucolic landscape surrounding him is filled with incredibly colorful details.

I've never been to Europe, but I've seen pictures. To me, this beautiful colored-glass collage surely rivals that of Notre Dame. As the impact of the initial beauty dissipates, my thoughts turn to the cost of heating such a vast arched-ceiling space in the winter.

Before I can get down to any hard calculations or concerns, a crisp voice calls out from the shadows.

"May I help you?"

When I turn, the sight that greets me feels as though it has been snatched directly from the blooper reel of *Keeping Mum*. The minister's face is almost a caricature. The image that next pops to mind is *Mr. Magoo in Hi-Fi*. A strange vinyl record my mother had in her collection.

Sensing a tidal wave of emotion rising at the thought of my deceased mom, I stuff it down with the deft skill of a seasoned foster kid and paste on a big smile.

"You certainly can. I'm Mitzy Moon." I extend my right hand as I walk toward the pastor.

His bulbous nose twitches, but there isn't a smile strong enough to lift his sagging cheeks. "Welcome to the First Methodist Church, Mrs. Moon."

I pull my hand back from his too-soft, clammy

grip and struggle not to wipe it off on my jeans. "Oh, it's just Miss. You may have been acquainted with my grandmother, Isadora—" For a minute I can't remember the surname of her fourth husband. Thankfully, the minister comes to my rescue.

"Isadora Willamet? Oh, she and Joe were such devoted congregants. I had heard the Lord called her home, but she wasn't a member of my flock at the time. The funeral services were held elsewhere. I pray our Lord welcomed her with open arms."

Doesn't seem like the right time to tell him she never made it to the pearly gates, and that he could express his condolences in person if he so chose. I wisely let it lie. "Yes, she very much enjoyed her time here. This is a beautiful little chapel."

His spine stiffens. "Sanctuary."

"Indeed." I'm not the person to get into an argument over the semantics of church-related room designations. "I was sorry to hear that someone vandalized your Nativity scene. Is there a reason it's still displayed in January?"

His brow furrows, and my psychic senses tingle with the heat of his judgment. "The Nativity scene remains on display through Epiphany. As I'm sure your grandmother told you, the gifts of the magi are bestowed on Epiphany. It would hardly be right to remove the Nativity prior to that momentous occasion."

"Of course. You're right." Yeesh!

An awkward silence hangs between us, and the mood ring on my left hand burns with a message.

Pretending to admire the *sanctuary* further, I turn and risk a surreptitious glance at the misty black cabochon.

The image reveals the minister behind the pulpit, in full Sunday regalia. Thanks for nothing! I've already deduced he's the pastor.

The minister clears his throat. "Is there anything else, *Miss* Moon?"

If I didn't know better, I'd almost think he was disappointed in me for being unmarried. Maybe it's time to try another tack. "Sheriff Harper asked me to look into things. I've had some success in the past—"

The cartoon character's entire expression changes and interrupts my flow. His heavily lidded eyes widen, his nostrils flare, and his lips finally find the strength to curve upwards. "Oh! You're that Mitzy Moon."

Swallowing my snarky response regarding the quantity of Mitzy Moons he assumes reside in this town, I nod and smile.

He ushers me toward a pew, and I take a seat on the less-than-comfortable wooden bench. "I was wondering if you made mention of the Nativity scene, in a special or important way, from the pulpit?"

His chinless jaw falls open, and he gazes at me with something akin to rapture. "So, it's true. The angels speak to you."

Oh, wow. This is the first I'm hearing this particular rumor, and I'm not entirely sure how to keep the abject shock from my face. "Mmhmm."

"Then I know our infant Lord and Savior is in good hands. The Sunday after the Lord's birth, I gave a sermon specifically addressing Epiphany. I always encourage folks to look at the coming year with fresh eyes and fresh hopes. Forgiving the transgressions of the previous year and celebrating the coming resurrection of our Lord."

Too much to unpack. I'll skip ahead. "Do you possibly have a list of the congregants that may have been at that after-Christmas service?"

His momentary lightness fades. "We don't take attendance."

"Of course not. It was a silly idea. I'm thinking maybe your message pricked the conscience of a specific congregant." Not being super familiar with religious jargon, I won't get much farther just continuing to repeat his words.

"Ah." He raises a finger and taps the side of his nose. "Mrs. Coleman can help you. The woman who plays the organ, and also serves as the church secretary. She took it upon herself to make an unofficial list of members who attend each week. We choose one name from the list of those who were with us every Sunday for an entire year, and then she and I attend Easter dinner at their home the following year. Our members consider it quite an honor." His grin returns.

Nod and smile. That's all I've got left. "All right. Perhaps if I could speak to Mrs. Coleman, and get a copy of that list, it would help me narrow the pool of suspects." As soon as I say the word, I know it was a poor choice.

His bushy grey-white eyebrows arch. "Suspects? In my congregation? Oh, Miss Moon, I assure you no one from this church had anything to do with this Nativity prank."

Time to get back on his good side. "I'm sure you're correct, Reverend. Although, it would certainly help me to know who's not responsible. Pin Cherry Harbor isn't a vast metropolis, but if I can at least start by ruling some folks out, it makes my job much easier. I'm sure you understand."

He sucks his bottom lip in between his teeth, and his thick eyelids lower as he contemplates my request. Finally, the minister leans forward and whispers, "If it's what the angels recommend."

Smiling, I manage to mumble an "Mmhmm,"

and he leads me through a side exit to the adjacent church offices.

The hallway seems dark and cave-like compared to the vast vaulted space we exited. He opens a door bearing the nameplate "Secretary," and the woman behind the desk looks up with a broad smile as we enter.

Teeth.

No matter how I try to reinterpret her face, all I see are teeth. The kind of chompers that surely garnered her the wrong type of attention when she was a schoolgirl. My heart goes out to her.

Carrying my own abnormally white mantle of hair through my school years had been an unwelcome burden. I'd been called many names, including *Powder* after the critically acclaimed movie, but, more often than not, ghost girl. If those kids only knew how prescient their comments had been.

Blerg. I zoned out and missed the introduction portion.

Mrs. Coleman is leaning over her desk with an eagerly outstretched hand and a slowly fading smile.

Lurching forward, I shove my hand in hers. "Sorry! I was reflecting on the gorgeous sanctuary and got distracted. I'm Mitzy Moon. Nice to meet you, Mrs. Coleman." When I attempt a deep breath, the cloying aroma wafting from the plethora of potpourri dishes nearly makes me gag.

She grips my hand with surprising strength and pumps it vigorously. "Hello. Hello, and welcome to the First Methodist Church of Pin Cherry Harbor. Are you applying for membership?"

The underwhelmed pastor fills her in on the nature of my visit, and Mrs. Coleman sucks a sharp breath in through her protruding teeth. "Golly! That theft caught me off guard. We've had that Nativity scene for almost forty years. Can you believe it?"

This feels like a question that doesn't need answering, so I nod and smile, and take shallow breaths.

"Well, I said, the whole world is going to H-E-double-hockey-sticks in a handbasket. So, I suppose I shouldn't have been so surprised. But you know how kids are these days. Just last month, we had an incident with two of our teenagers smoking outside Bible study. They just snuck out through a side door and they were hiding under the eaves of this very church. So bold!"

Thankfully, the reverend puts an end to her report. "Mrs. Coleman, I am sure Miss Moon has a busy agenda. If you could simply provide her with your special list from the Sunday before the theft, she will be on her way and can begin her investigation."

Mrs. Coleman seems to have heard my name and the purpose of my visit for the first time.

"Oh, my goodness! You're Isadora Willamet's granddaughter! Why, the ladies at bingo—"

I shake a finger. "You know what they say about gossip, Mrs. Coleman."

Her eyes widen and her jaw hangs open, revealing the full extent of her impressive front teeth.

Insulting the woman who holds the potential key to my case was not my intention, but she doesn't get my sense of humor. Offering an over-the-top wink, I try to save the exchange. "Only the good parts are true!"

Her entire expression lights up, and she throws a hand over her mouth as she gasps. Then she proceeds to repeat the entire joke—out loud. "You know what they say about gossip, only the good parts are true! That's so funny. Oh, my goodness, wait till I tell the ladies what a hoot you are."

There seems to be a richly fed rumor mill running behind the scenes in my beloved new hometown. It doesn't hurt to scoop a little truth in every once in a while. Maybe it will even out.

"Honestly, aren't you the best? Could I get that list?" My lungs are screaming for un-perfumed air.

The minister seems to have reached his fill of

meaningless chatter. "I shall leave you two ladies. You're in good hands, Miss Moon. My condolences for your grandmother."

"Thank you. I'll tell her you said that."

His thick, weighted eyelids peel back and he mumbles what must be a protective passage of Scripture under his breath as he sneaks out of the room.

I'd love to smack myself on the forehead for that slip-up, but I'd rather not draw any additional attention to it. Thankfully, Mrs. Coleman is busy rifling through her desk drawers in search of the requested list and seems to have missed the potential gossip goldmine.

"That's the strangest thing."

"What is?"

She pushes the last drawer closed and looks at me with utter confusion. "I can't find that week's list."

My claircognizance seems to snatch a word from the ether, and my silly old mouth shouts it out without thinking. "Stolen?"

She gasps, and her teeth once again take center stage. "Stolen? Why, I don't think so. Someone had to come in— It's just not done."

"It's possible that the person who removed the baby Jesus from the manger knew you kept the lists in your top drawer. Maybe they took the doll and the list."

A deep crease forms between her eyebrows, and she shakes her head violently. "Doll! The replica of the baby Jesus in the manger is no *doll*. And no one in our congregation would stoop to thieving. From the church office, no less. Not on your life. I probably had one of my senior moments and put it in the wrong file. Just give me a couple of minutes."

"I didn't mean to offend, Mrs. Coleman. Would you mind if I step back into the sanctuary and take another look at that stained-glass mural?"

Her expression immediately softens, and I hope I'm back on the gossip girl's good side. "Of course, dear. I'm sure that list will turn up in a minute and I'll bring you a copy."

"Thank you."

Slipping out of the cloud of potpourri-tainted air perfuming her office, I let my fingers bounce from the back of one pew to the next as I walk to the rear of the sanctuary for the best view of the stained glass.

As my left hand drags across the last pew, a whisper tingles up my arm and tickles my eardrum.

"Child."

Child? If that pew and my ring are trying to tell me that a child removed the baby from the manger, that could be a lead. But a child would hardly be wily enough to swipe the attendance list.

Stepping toward the center, I gaze up at the magnificent work of art.

When I pull my eyes away and return to the side door, it opens unexpectedly.

Mrs. Coleman bustles through, a bundle of nerves. "I'm so sorry, Miss Moon, but I can't find that list anywhere. I hate to think that you're right, but what if someone did take it?"

"Let's hope not. Does the list change all that much from week to week?"

She taps her fingernails on her teeth, and I have to bite my tongue to keep from saying something. Her gaze travels up and bounces from left to right as she scans her memory. "Well, the Sunday before would've been the official Christmas service, and that's always very well attended. The following Sunday would've had a much smaller crowd."

"Do you have the list from the Christmas service?"

She smiles, and the effort squeezes her eyes to slits. "Yes. That one is in my top drawer with all the others."

I'd hate to point out that "all" is a tad incorrect. "Could you make me a copy of that list? Maybe you could go through it and cross off anyone you remember not attending the next week. At least it would give me something to start with."

She claps her hands together and gives a little hop. "I'll hop right to it. You're as smart as a whip." Mrs. Coleman opens the door to return to her office and glances back to see if I'm following.

"I'll wait here. I don't want to interrupt your concentration."

The secretary points her finger at me and winks. "You are plum full of great ideas."

I hate to break it to her that the great idea has more to do with her office being *plum full* of potpourri than my brain spilling over with genius plans. However, no harm, no foul.

Less than five minutes later, she returns with a photocopy of the Christmas service list. More than half the names have been crossed out.

"Wow! Attendance really drops off after the holidays."

She bends her head and presses the palms of her hands together in prayer pose. "Everyone finds the Lord in their own way. Pastor always says, 'deeds not creeds.' So I can only hope that these poor souls are spending the rest of their Sundays doing good deeds, and that our dear Lord will take note of their good works."

I shake the list once and press my lips together. "Copy that. Thanks for the list." Turning to exit the church through the sanctuary, Mrs. Coleman's voice stops me in my tracks.

"You don't have to go back through the sanctuary, dear. This hallway leads you to a side exit right into the parking lot."

Nodding my thanks, I head down the hallway when a sudden question comes to mind. "Is this door always unlocked?"

Her megawatt smile beams down the hallway. "The Lord's house is open to all."

"Understood."

I push open the door and step onto the sidewalk. It's impossible not to notice the looming Nativity scene, mere feet from my current location. It would only take a second to hop over and grab the baby Jesus. If he weren't already missing.

The empty manger gapes at me, refusing to offer any additional clues.

CHAPTER 4

EASING MY FATHER'S TRUCK back onto the main road, I'm grateful for Artie, the town snowplow operator. I'm not sure how she does it, but she keeps the roads beautifully clear despite this year's near-constant snowfall. My winter driving skills have definitely improved since my first frosty months in almost-Canada, but I still prefer a clear road to one covered by snow with possible dangerous ice lurking beneath.

On the seat next to me the phone rings, and when I catch sight of the name on caller ID, I nearly veer into a snowdrift! Quince Knudsen is *calling* me? As in, not a one-word text. I'm getting a phone call where he'll be required to use at least a handful of words!

Must be important. I hit the speaker icon. "Hey, Quince, what's up?"

"I need to talk."

The sharp edge of emotion in his voice cuts through the phone. "What's going on? Are you in danger? Where are you?"

"Bookshop."

To be fair, I did ask a lot of questions in rapid succession, and there was virtually no chance that he would answer all of them. He picked the most important one and got straight to the point. "Understood. I'm just leaving the First Methodist Church. Do you want to meet at the diner?"

"No. Private."

"Copy that. I'll be there shortly."

And he's gone. A little part of me expected a "bye" or possibly an affirmative grunt, but I get it. The communication was finished in his mind. He'll save his possible verbosity for when he sees me face-to-face.

Doubling down on the advantage of a plowed road, I push the boundaries of what would be considered a safe speed and hustle back to the bookstore.

There's no time for fancy parking or garage codes.

I swerve across the lane of oncoming traffic, which is empty, so don't worry, and park against the curb in front of the Bell, Book & Candle. Jumping out of the truck, I risk a brisk jog to the front door.

Big mistake.

Five seconds into my brave pseudo-sprint, I hit a patch of ice and go down like a pyramid of toilet paper in a grocery store that met its match in a speeding cart.

Unfortunately, I fall forward and crack my denim-clad knee pretty solidly against the icy sidewalk. Slowly getting back on my feet, I hobble toward my beautiful hand-carved front door, but don't have time to admire it.

Inside the high-ceilinged shop, the massive chandelier glitters warmly. The cantankerous mood ring on my left hand stabs an icy circle around my finger. Glancing down, I see the vast expanse of a frozen lake. Great clue, ring. There are only about a million of those in Birch County!

"Hey. I need your help." Quince is agitated, and his usual lackadaisical expression and drooped shoulders are all tense and pinched.

"What's going on?"

"It's my uncle."

This is the first I'm hearing of an uncle. "On your dad's side?"

"Yah. My uncle Quade was murdered."

Under intense pressure, I have two modes: dark humor or impulsive action. Thankfully, the "act without thinking" takes over and I throw my arms around the young man and squeeze tightly. "I'm so sorry. When did this happen? Are the police looking into it?"

Quince is extraordinarily uncomfortable with my show of affection. He wiggles out of my hug and shoves both of his hands in the pockets of his jeans. "This morning. They said it's an accident."

Wow. This puts me in an awkward position. I'm eager to help Quince find out what's actually happened to his uncle, but it sounds like I'll have to directly defy my boyfriend's authority. "Sheriff Harper doesn't think it was murder?"

"Yah."

The unspoken part of the response is that Quince clearly doesn't agree. "I understand. Why do you think there was foul play?"

"My uncle went fishing every morning after the first milking. He's meticulous, like OCD meticulous. Same pattern. Time. And he doesn't drink."

The length of the speech gives me pause, and I wonder if there's a way to question the young man without making him feel judged. "So, I'm totally going to help you. Let's just get that part out of the way. But if you want me to do my job properly, I'm gonna have to ask some tough questions. It may seem like I'm doubting your story, or siding with the cops, but I'm not. I just need to make sure I understand. All right?"

He nods and swipes at his nose with the back of his hand.

"You said your uncle was meticulous. And you said something about milking? Can you explain?"

His hands fidget in his pockets and his shoulders shrug almost imperceptibly.

Biting my tongue, I wait for what I hope is additional information.

"He's younger than my dad. Divorced. He just does things in a particular way."

"Got it. And what about the milking?"

"He's a cheesemaker."

And here goes my brain. The second he says cheesemaker, all I can think of is *Monty Python*. "Blessed are the cheesemakers." Don't worry, I don't say it out loud. "Got it. So he milks his cows, I'm assuming, and then he goes ice fishing? Every morning?"

"Yah. He calls it his thinking time."

"So, this morning he milked the cows, headed out to the fishing house, and when he didn't come back after his thinking time, who called it in?"

"My dad."

"How did your dad know he wasn't back?"

"Breakfast."

Sadly, Quince is slipping back toward monosyllabic territory, and I'm having to rely on my extra senses to pull details out of thin air. "So your dad and his brother have breakfast together every morning?"

"Yah."

"Got it. This morning your uncle didn't show up, and did your dad go out to the icehouse?"

The young man can't bring himself to speak. Emotion twists his face as he nods.

"Your dad discovered the body?" There's no need for him to answer. "I'm so sorry. Did he call the police?"

Quince pulls his hands from his pockets, crosses his arms, and squeezes himself as a response.

The only sound in the bookshop is the wind whipping up from the great lake nestled in our harbor and buffeting the brick exterior.

"I heard it on the scanner." His voice catches and he looks away.

"Oh, man. That sucks. Again, I'm so sorry." I'm starting to sound like a broken record, but my heart is breaking for this kid. "You mentioned murder. What makes you think that?"

"Sheriff said Quade passed out, the fire burned out, and he froze to death."

Sorry, Erick, but if I'd been at the crime scene, I would've said this to your face. "They wouldn't have the medical examiner's report already. That sounds like a pure guess."

Quince looks up with pleading hazel eyes. "I know, right?"

"I'll talk to Erick. I can get a copy of the ME's report. In the meantime, can you show me the way to the icehouse?"

"Yah."

The somber drive out to the lake where Quince's uncle's body was discovered is wrapped in a heavy blanket of silence.

My curious mind is churning over the few details I possess, and I can't seem to let go of one burning question. I brave a quick query. "Are you named after your uncle or something? I mean, Q names aren't that common."

He gazes out the window, and his finger traces abstract patterns in the frost forming on the inside of the glass. "It's a family thing. My dad's name is Quintin." He sighs. "I suppose, if I have kids—"

This particular tradition seems more of a burden than a gift, but I'm so happy to have a family after six plus years in foster care, I'd embrace practically anything. Quincy, or, as I call him, Quince, Quintin, and Quade. I'm wondering when this tradition started, what other odd "Q" names I would find hanging on the Knudsen family tree if I were to climb any higher. Maybe I'd have to shimmy down lower? I don't know. I'm not a genealogy expert.

Quince gestures to the left, and I turn down an access road that parallels the shoreline of a frozen body of water. A small wooden structure, barely five foot by five foot and painted sky-blue, comes into view.

"That's it." He points to the shack.

Several sets of tracks mark the snow cover near the edge of the lake. I pull in as far as I dare, and we jump out of the truck.

The heavy clouds of the morning have blown free, and an incongruent bright-blue sky and white-gold winter sun gleam above the sparkling powder-covered ice.

We walk toward the icehouse wrapped with yellow tape that proclaims. "CRIME SCENE KEEP OUT."

When we get closer, I notice a large piece of paper taped to the crime-scene tape. On the white sheet, written in thick black permanent marker, is the phrase, "This means you, Mitzy."

"Rude."

Quince shrugs. "He knows I know you."

It's hard not to notice that the kid avoids using the term friends. Clearly, that's far too familiar for this young man. "Yeah, and he also knows I'm a bit of a snoop."

Quince turns to head back toward the truck.

"Hey, where are you going?"

He looks over his shoulder and scrunches up his face in confusion. "It says keep out."

I laugh out loud and put a hand to my stomach to aid in containing the hilarity. "Look, kid, it's a cute sign and all, but it's not going to keep me from investigating this case."

For the first time since I found him moping in my bookshop, his face lights up. "Sweet."

"Also, before I forget. You said something about your uncle not being a drinker. Why did that come up?"

"My dad said they found an empty bourbon bottle next to his chair."

"Oh, that's why Erick said Quade 'passed out.' Are you sure about the drinking?"

"No alcohol with his meds. Hasn't had a drink in over ten years."

"Copy that."

I circle around the icehouse, feeling for clues. This is one time where Quince's silence comes in handy. I need the quiet to focus and reach out with my extra abilities.

No sign of forced entry, but as soon as I turn my

focus toward the door, my clairaudience grabs the word *screw* floating on the breeze.

Taking two careful steps closer to the door, I notice a small hole just above the lock mechanism. I turn to my cohort and attempt to confirm my other-worldly information. "If someone put a screw right here"—I point to the mark—"would that prevent the lock from opening from the inside?"

Quince leans forward, squeezes his eyes, and chews the inside of his cheek. "I think so."

Now it's time for me to use my moody mood ring as a divining rod. A little trick I learned on another snow-covered case.

Crouching down, I remove my glove, hold my hand over the snow, and focus on the screw.

At first, the results are dismal.

Taking another deep breath, I attempt to visualize the screw being knocked loose by an overeager deputy—I'm assuming Deputy Paulsen. I have to pull my focus back and not be distracted by my dislike for her overbearing tactics.

A sudden heat emanates from my ring and my hand pulls to the right. The heat lessens as I move it too far.

I ease my fingers left and the heat increases. Making minuscule adjustments, I find the position where the heat around my ring finger is most intense and then plunge my bare hand into the freezing snow.

To his credit, Quince has remained utterly silent the entire time.

My fingers sting and burn with cold. Only my determination to help my friend pushes my numb fingers deeper.

Eureka!

Clumsily pinching my frozen digits around the screw, I extract it from the icy crystals and smile triumphantly. "Um, you wouldn't happen to have an evidence bag, would you?"

He shakes his head. "Film can?"

"That'll work."

Quince digs in the pocket of his coat and extracts the empty film canister. He pops off the lid and I drop the screw in for safekeeping. He presses on the lid and hands the canister to me.

I shake my head and lift my hands in the air as though it's a holdup. "I'm not supposed to be here, remember?"

A half grin lifts one side of his mouth and he nods. "I'll go see Sheriff Harper. Won't mention you."

Chuckling, I shake my head. "It's all right. You can say whatever you need to. There's probably not any recoverable evidence on that thing, but the fact that someone put a screw into the fish house to purposely jam the lock mechanism should at least make them reconsider cause of death."

Tears well up in the corners of his eyes, and I'm afraid his eyelids could freeze shut.

"We should get back in the truck. Come on." My clairsentience picks up on a wave of relief. I know he's grateful. I don't need him to cry to prove that.

The drive back into town is as silent as the drive out to the lake, but this quiet feels different—it's protecting a fragile hope.

We found something. And this is the way every case unravels. One thing leads to the next thing, which leads to the next thing, and, eventually, if you find enough things, you find the bad guy (or gal) and you can put them away.

Stopping in front of the bookshop, I glance toward my passenger and grin. "You should probably walk down to the station on your own. If I pull up in front and let you out, you're going to be fresh out of plausible deniability."

His laughter warms my heart, and he thanks me as he slips out of the truck and trudges up Main Street.

Dutiful daughter that I am, I fill up my dad's gas tank and park his truck back in his garage. I also tuck the keys under the visor, where I found them.

Before this case takes off, I better see about getting a new vehicle to replace my "retired" Jeep.

After I let myself in through the heavy metal door leading from the alleyway between my building and my dad's, I stomp the snow off my boots and acknowledge the shocking realization that I have no idea how one buys a car.

Time for a spirited consultation.

Grams has been spending a lot of time on the third floor of the printing museum. Rather than risk calling out her name and drawing Twiggy's wrath, I sashay through the "Employees Only" door leading from the bookshop into the adjacent exhibitions and trudge up to the third floor.

Her pensive expression and frantic writing worry me, but when I see the mountain of loose sheets in the trash barrel, serious concern sets in.

"Grams, is everything all right?"

A luminous head swivels toward the disruption and, I kid you not, actual ghost flames are flickering from her eyes.

"Never mind. Never mind. I can figure out how to buy a car by myself."

The pen clatters to the floor, and she zooms toward me. A sparkling blur of apologies. "I'm so sorry, sweetie. I've had writer's block for days, and I finally solved my story problem. My emotions are running high and interfering with my ability to grip things. I keep dropping the pen. I can't write as fast as the thoughts are coming to me—"

"Easy, girl. Sounds like a lot of ghost problems."

Fortunately, my joke lands and she laughs with relief. "Thanks, I needed that."

"Can I ask which part of the story is giving you problems? I thought you were writing memoirs. Seems like there would only be one version of those." Crossing my arms, I tilt my head and scrunch up one corner of my mouth as I wait for her to defend her obvious creative license.

"Oh, it's not important, dear. You said something about buying a car. I left you the Jeep and the Mercedes. Do you really need a third car?"

"Thing is, ever since the Jeep got hot-wired—" I pause and wait for her to nod in acknowledgment. "—she's had a whole host of problems. And she left me stranded in front of the dry cleaners. Luckily, I have a resourceful boyfriend who rescued me and took care of the problem. But, as you know, I prefer to be an independent woman."

She presses a shimmering hand to her ample bosom and laughs so hard she ghost snorts. "Understatement of this century, my dear."

Grinning mischievously, I meet her on her own terms. "People tell me I take after my dearly departed grandmother."

She winks. "Touché, as you're always saying."

"So, back to my thing about needing to buy a car. I actually really liked the Jeep, and I'm not opposed to getting another one. I just don't know where to go or what questions to ask."

Grams nods her head and adjusts one of her strands of pearls. "Oh, I know just what you mean. People often take advantage of a woman shopping for big-ticket items on her own. I found Silas Willoughby to be an incredibly useful bit of arm candy."

Now it's my turn to laugh until tears leak from my eyes. "Silas! Arm candy!" I have to bend over and support myself by placing my hands on my knees. The imagery flashing through my head is enough to make me pass out from my attack of the giggles.

Grams places a fist on her Marchesa-clad hip. "Well, arm candy might not be the right phrase, exactly, but you know what I mean. Call Silas. He'll know what to do."

"Thank you for helping me with my problem. Is there anything I can do to help you with yours?"

If ghosts could look guilty . . .

"What? Oh, don't trouble yourself. I'll figure it out. All in a day's work, I suppose."

"If you say so, Isadora."

I hurry toward the stairs and attempt to distance myself from the apparition before the inevitable thought pops into my head. A day's work? Has Isadora ever done a day's work?

An offended retort echoes down the stairwell. "I heard that, young lady."

"Get out of my head, woman!" Our shared laughter warms my heart.

CHAPTER 5

I LEARNED a new expression when I arrived in Pin Cherry Harbor: stuck in my craw. I have no idea what it means, but, at this moment, it feels right. That's exactly where my grandmother's advice is wedged.

It's not that I doubt the powers of the mysterious attorney/alchemist Silas Willoughby, but he drives a 1908 Ford Model T! If that was the last time he was wheeling and dealing for a new vehicle, I'm not sure he's the right man for the job. However, I will not be the girl who has to have her boyfriend hold her hand for every major life decision. If I'm flipping a coin, it's coming up Silas. Traipsing across the thick carpets in my swanky apartment, I flop down on the bed to make the call.

A hiss and a tan streak shoot out from under the frame as it creaks.

"Pyewacket! Geez! You scared me half to death! But I suppose I frightened you too. I'm sorry, Mr. Cuddlekins. Please come back and let me apologize properly."

Pyewacket's broad head and sharply tufted black ears peer around the edge of the door to my enormous closet. His large golden eyes squint, and waves of suspicion roll off him.

"I swear, I didn't know you were under the bed. I would never launch an attack against such a powerful adversary."

"Reow." Can confirm. He struts toward me and his thick stubby tail flicks with irritation, or maybe it's tolerance. The hairs on the back of my neck tingle, and I'm certain tolerance is the correct word. He gracefully launches onto the thick down comforter, circles once, and flops down facing away from me.

"I accept my punishment, oh furry master. Now, I have to call Silas and convince him to help me buy a car. Any advice?"

Pye yawns widely and exposes his dangerous fangs. His large head hits the bed with a thud and lolls toward me. One golden eye meets my gaze. "Ree-ow." Soft but condescending.

"Thanks for nothing, buddy."

. . .

Cut to—

Silas riding shotgun in my father's truck as we drive toward Broken Rock. There is a dealership there that he's fond of visiting. However, no matter how I phrase the question, I'm unable to discern whether he's ever actually purchased a vehicle from this location.

When I pull into the parking lot, my eyes wander up and down the scant rows of vehicles. They don't look exactly new. "Silas, is this a used car lot? I mean, not to be this girl, but can't I afford a new car?"

He harrumphs and smooths his great bushy mustache with a thumb and forefinger. "I am certain the estate your grandmother left you could purchase many new cars. I find used vehicles to be more discreet for your—line of work—for lack of a better word."

"Line of work? It's not like I'm a lady of the night, to use your terminology. I'm an amateur snoop. What does it matter what kind of car I drive?"

He steeples his fingers and bounces his chin thoughtfully on the tips of his pointers.

Blerg. I've earned myself a lesson. He's not

giving me any instruction, so I best take some deep breaths and tune in to psychic radio.

Stilling my spinning mind, I reach out with all of my extrasensory perceptions. Why am I seeing the dive bar Final Destination? Clarity rockets in and I slap my hand on my thigh. "You're right. Some of my undercover missions wouldn't have gone as well as they did if I were driving a fancy new car. Sorry I doubted you. Although, let me be clear, I'm no mechanic. If something goes wrong with this not-quite-new car, I can't always be calling Erick to bail me out."

A satisfied grin widens beneath his grey lip warmer and he nods. "Once we've completed our transaction, remind me to introduce you to Clarence."

The name means absolutely nothing to me. "Do I know Clarence?"

The satisfied smile fades instantly, and my mentor shakes his head. "One would not be introduced to an individual with whom one was already acquainted."

"You're not wrong." Sparing myself any further humiliation, I open my door and exit the truck. On the drive over, I was instructed to act disinterested and only point out flaws. Apparently, this is an important part of the negotiation strategy.

Tromping down the first row of vehicles, a

lovely Jeep, very similar to my previous vehicle, catches my eye. "Cool! This is exactly what I want, Silas."

He glances toward me with furrowed brows and my claircognizance knows in an instant I've disappointed him greatly.

An eager salesman jogs our way. He smiles brightly at me, but when he catches sight of Silas, his entire persona shifts.

Maybe my old alchemist is the perfect shopping partner.

"Hi, Mr. Willoughby. Just looking?"

Silas smooths his mustache and lets the man simmer in a moment of silence. "One is always looking prior to a decision. Are they not?"

The frustrated salesman smiles weakly and changes his tactic. "What about you, Miss? You see anything you like?"

Still recovering from my recent scolding, I gesture toward the Jeep I truly desire and attempt to *neg*. A term I learned from my young stepbrother. "Those don't look like snow tires."

The salesman is clearly eager to move things along and get us inside the warm building to sign papers. "Good eye, Miss. That vehicle came to us late in the fall, and we weren't planning on putting snow tires on her unless she sold this winter. You take her off the lot today, and I'll put on a brand-new set of tires for a hundred bucks."

I smile and open my mouth, but the voice that responds is not mine.

"Oh, come now, we both know you don't have a set of brand-new snow tires on the lot. I'm certain any tires you placed on this vehicle would have a minimum of 10,000 miles on their belts."

On their belts, under their belts . . . Silas is crafty.

The salesman shrugs. "You got me there, Mr. Willoughby. We'll put snow tires on, no charge."

Color me impressed. This negotiating thing is harder than it looks. "How many miles does she have on her?" I've heard guys ask that question.

The salesman nods. "Let me check."

He moves to the vehicle, turns the key to the accessory position and glances at the odometer. "Just under 80,000. Which is mint condition for a vintage Jeep."

Nice. I like that he didn't use the word old. Vintage has much more panache.

Silas clears his throat and steps toward the vehicle. "How can we be sure that the odometer hasn't rolled over? Do you have a list of previous owners? If it's a single-owner vehicle, I'd be inclined to accept your supposition. However, if this is a multi-owner vehicle, I feel it's likely 180,000, good sir."

The salesman's lips are turning blue, and my own teeth are beginning a subtle chatter.

"Let's head inside and take a look at the paperwork."

I eagerly fall in line behind him, but Silas grips my arm.

"We shall peruse the remaining rows and meet you inside. That should give you plenty of time to assemble the necessary documents."

The salesman nods and hustles indoors.

As soon as he's out of earshot, I pitch a tiny fit. "Silas! I want this Jeep. It's four-wheel drive. I like this shade of green, and 80,000 miles is not that many."

"Would you marry the first man who asked you?"

The question hits me out of nowhere. Instantly, I'm picturing the first proposal I ever received back in Arizona. It was after a particularly intense night of partying and I honestly only remember the guy's last name. I think it was Centers. That can't be right. That's not a name, is it? Blerg. I don't even remember his last name.

Silas and his smug grin annoy me.

"All right. You win. I wouldn't— I didn't. Let's see what else they have."

He leads me on a serpentine tour of the small

lot. In the end, he finds a slightly newer Jeep, a beautiful shade of blue, with lovely snow tires.

As I admire the car with sparkling eyes, Silas chuckles. "You see, vehicles in the front row are the ones they *need* to move. The hidden gems are tucked away. This car is in excellent condition and they surely paid too much for it. This will provide an invigorating negotiation, but I believe the car will serve you well. Would you not agree?"

There's that phrasing again. Yes, I would not agree? No, I would not agree? As I place my hand on the front fender, a feeling of warmth and belonging radiates up my arm. My eyes widen with surprise and I glance toward Silas.

His proud grin says it all.

My mentor seems to be a couple steps ahead of me, despite my special gifts. "You're right, as usual. Now can we go inside and get a hot cup of coffee?"

"Indeed."

When we trudge indoors, the salesman is still rifling through paperwork on his desk.

Silas approaches and drops silently into one of the two chairs. "We have chosen the 1997 Jeep Cherokee with snow tires in the back row. Our offer is 3500 even."

The salesman drops the papers on his desk and looks aghast. "That's less than we paid for it. I can't let it off the lot for less than 4500."

Silas chuckles and leans back in his chair.

My mood ring gives me nothing, but I swear I can feel the number 3000 in the air. The salesman is lying! They only paid 3000 for that vehicle, and Silas must know it. I cross my arms and lean back like my trainer—ready to wait this guy out.

His gaze bounces back and forth like a tennis ball at Wimbledon. "I got to talk to my manager."

Silas nods. "By all means."

The man rises from his chair and vanishes into a back room.

I've watched this scene in so many movies, and I never believed a second of it. Is this actually how business is done? What a racket. I suppose you can't judge an entire industry by one experience, but stereotypes exist for a reason.

The salesman returns with an older version of himself in tow.

Oh dear, this is a family-owned business, and daddy is not happy with his son's performance.

The older gentleman has a salt-and-pepper mustache which pales in comparison to the one Silas is rocking. Although, Sales Daddy's beer belly is significantly larger.

"I understand you're interested in the '97 Cherokee. That vehicle is in excellent condition and we definitely can't let her off the lot for less than 4200."

Hold on! The price came down by $300 in under two minutes. I'm starting to understand how this game works. Before Silas can reply, I double down on our offer. "I believe we offered 3500, all in."

I feel a little burst of pride from my mentor.

Sales Daddy shakes his head, leans toward his son and mumbles something he clearly hopes is inaudible.

Lucky for me, I have extra audible.

Junior takes the ball. "I'm sure you're on a tight budget, Miss. We're willing to go as low as $4000. And I'll include taxes and registration."

I wait for Silas to reply, but he seems to be interested in continuing the experiment with me at the helm.

Shaking my head, I cross my arms and lean away. "You hit the nail on the head. I can't go a penny over $3500. That's my final offer."

Sales Daddy jumps in. "We need to look at some paperwork. Give us a minute."

I lift my eyebrows as though I couldn't care less, and shrug.

The two men retreat into the back room, and I risk a glance at Silas. He smooths his mustache with thumb and forefinger and nods his approval. A soft phrase reaches my ears, even though I don't see his lips move. *Be ready to walk out.*

My jaw drops a little, but I nod.

The father-son team returns. Daddy takes the lead. "The best we can do is $3800. You're basically robbing us at that price. I won't even be able to pay his commission."

Pushing myself up from the chair, I smile pleasantly. "I would think you'd have your own son on a profit-sharing program in a family-run business, but who's to say. I'm sorry we weren't able to come to an agreement."

I walk toward the door, and Silas follows. If I didn't know better, I'd say he's gleeful.

My hand is on the push bar, and I'm a second from exiting.

Junior calls out. "Hold on. Hold on. I'll take the loss. You can have it for 3500, all in, like you said."

As I turn to respond, Silas offers me a surreptitious wink and I nearly squeal. "That sounds great. Let's draw up the papers." I'm not sure if draw up the papers is the right phrase, but who cares! I just bought my first car! And I got a heck of a deal.

CHAPTER 6

I WON'T BORE you with the endless contract
signing details . . . Sometime later, I'm the proud
new owner of a vintage Jeep. Silas offers to drive the
new purchase back to the bookshop, and I return
my father's truck to his garage. Now that I've handled practicalities, it seems like the perfect opportunity to meet my boyfriend for a casual dinner and
pump him for information on the Knudsen case.

Lying on the padded mahogany bench in my
home for vintage couture, I stare at the cedar-lined
ceiling in the closet. The phone is on speaker and
the call rings through.

The sheriff's confident, warm voice fills the
space. "Hey, did you already solve the case of the
missing baby Jesus?"

Whoopsie. Once I got my teeth into the murder, I forgot I was supposed to be working for Erick. "I've got some good leads. How about you? Any interesting cases?"

His deep chuckle makes my tummy flip. "I wasn't born yesterday, Moon. Meet me at the diner in five, and I'll give you an update on Quince's uncle."

"Am I really that transparent?"

"Not at all. But there is a certain predictability to your—shall we call it—snoopiness?"

"Wow, just wow. I think that comment is going to cost you a free dinner. Looks like you're buying now, Sheriff."

"Not a problem. See ya soon."

The call ends, and I lazily push myself to a sitting position. Silas forced me into a "decent blouse" for our sales excursion. Now I have a fashion conundrum. Part of me wants to slip on a snarky T-shirt, but a smaller part of me wants to impress Erick.

I unbutton an additional button on the blouse and wink at myself in the mirror.

"Finally!"

Nearly jumping out of my skin, I clutch at my heart. "Grams! What have I told you about scaring the bejeezus out of me? Slow. Sparkly. Re-entry. Only. Please!"

"There wasn't time. I was afraid you were going

to lose the fashion battle and slip into your old ways. I'm so proud to see that you're finally paying attention to all my lessons. That blouse is delightful on you, and a little cleavage never hurts."

I blush self-consciously, and my hand reaches toward the button I just loosed.

"Don't worry, sweetie. Your secret is safe with me."

My eyes roll of their own accord, and I attempt to keep my thoughts regarding her finely honed gossip skills to myself.

Epic fail.

"Listen, young lady. My connections and access to information have helped you several times. Don't look a gift horse in the mouth."

The old adage makes me chuckle. "I really don't think of you as a horse, Grams, but you definitely are a gift."

Shimmering ghost tears spring to the corners of her eyes. "Oh, Mitzy."

I quickly raise an admonishing finger. "Don't you dare cry! I'll be forced to go to the cemetery, exhume you, and shove a handkerchief in your coffin!"

Her expression turns to shock. "Do you think that would work? Gosh, I was able to pick the ghost age I wanted, but I can't change my clothes. Do you think you could put outfits in there?

Maybe I could have a summer dress, a pant suit . . ."

I slip out of the closet before she can force me to make good on my empty threat. It's only a half-baked theory I've been playing with. It's not like I ran it past Silas or anything. As the bookcase door slides open, she's still rambling on about possible afterlife fashion choices.

Erick is already tucked into the corner booth, but, as I approach, he hops up to help me off with my coat.

"Thank you. If you're trying to butter me up for additional details about the empty manger, I hate to disappoint. I'm pretty convinced someone from the congregation took it, but until I can come up with motive, I'm going to have a hard time narrowing down the suspect list."

He slides back into the booth, and I sit opposite. He walks his fingers across the table, turns his palm up, and I slide my hand into his. It feels like home. And I very much like *home*.

Tally sidles up and, for once, her hands are empty. Her tightly wound, flame-red bun tilts from side to side as she offers each of us a broad smile. "What can I getcha? Coffee? Iced tea? Maybe a hot cocoa with whipped cream?"

"I'll take the last one!"

Erick smiles. "Me too."

There's no need to order food. My grandfather, Odell, is already hard at work on the grill. It never made sense to me before, but maybe the reason he always knows exactly what his customers want is because he's a little psychic. Silas thinks I inherited my gifts from my grandmother, but she only has visions. Some people call it clairvoyance. I have all the psychic senses and maybe one or more of them came from Odell Johnson. Food for thought.

Erick's free hand is slowly waving back and forth in front of my face and I bite my lip and wipe my eyes. "What did I miss?"

"I was telling you all about the Knudsen case. You missed everything. Too bad. Looks like our food is on the way. I won't have time to repeat the story."

"Erick Harper!"

Odell sets a beautiful burger and fries in front of me, and meatloaf with mashed potatoes in front of Erick. "Everything okay here?"

Before my smart aleck boyfriend can defend himself, I jump in and throw him under the bus. "Not even. Erick is refusing to share information about a case, but I have my ways."

Odell snickers too quickly. "I'd say. So my favorite granddaughter is on another case, eh?"

It's so strange to hear him say it. *Granddaughter.* Of course, it's literally some of the best news I've gotten in a long time. Most family secrets are meant to stay buried, but this one is definitely thriving in the light of day.

"I'm looking into the missing baby Jesus—"

"And she's not so secretly working for Quincy Knudsen. So, she's also looking into Quade's murder."

I gasp softly. "So it was murder."

He nods solemnly. "I had my suspicions. I was honestly just trying to spare Quintin's feelings, you know?"

I did know. I do know. "I get that."

Odell raps his knuckles twice on the silver-flecked white-Formica table, winks at me, and returns to the kitchen.

Pulling up my shoulders in anticipation, I bait the hook. "I have exciting news. So I'm going to be magnanimous and let you eat while I tell you my story."

Erick's big blue eyes widen with mock shock. "Is the news that you're not well? Because I've never seen you resist a plate of french fries."

In order to teach him a lesson, I shove several fries in my mouth and arch an eyebrow.

"I give up, Moon. Tell me your news." He picks up a fork and digs into his juicy meatloaf.

I fill him in on my car buying adventures and my expert negotiating skills.

He calmly swallows his food, wipes his mouth, and smiles. "Sounds like Silas is an excellent teacher. I know the dealership you're talking about in Broken Rock, and that father-son duo is a tough act to beat. Good for you. Did Silas introduce you to Clarence?"

It shouldn't surprise me that Erick knows Clarence. Pin Cherry is a rather small town. "Don't tell me you know him too?"

"Oh, for sure. He's helped me out with the Nova many times. What he doesn't know about cars isn't worth knowing. And he's fair as the day is long. You're in good hands with him."

"Well, that's two ringing endorsements from a couple of the people I trust most."

Erick smiles. "Good to know."

"Oh, don't let it go to your head, Sheriff."

He chuckles, and the remainder of our meal falls into silence as we devour our delicious suppers.

"All right, that's my news, Sheriff. What do you have for me?"

His eyes twinkle, and my extra senses pick up on his inner battle.

"If you're toying with the idea of baiting me further, *Ricky*. I'd advise against it."

His ready laughter is exactly what I'm hoping

for when I use his mother's pet name. To be fair, some of his old high school chums also call him Ricky, but, in general, with the status he holds in the community, people call him Erick, Mr. Harper, or, mostly, Sheriff.

"Sorry, Moon. Sadly, there isn't much to report yet. Because of the frozen nature of the—"

"Say body, don't say the other word."

He nods and presses his lips together in grim acknowledgment of the corpse. "Because of the frozen nature of the body, and the unusual sixty-degree temperature drop last night, the medical examiner has to send specimens to the state crime lab for verification. Her initial findings estimate time of death between midnight and 3:00 a.m. However, Mr. Knudsen claims he received a text from his brother at 5:30 a.m., confirming that the first milking was complete and their breakfast appointment was on after fishing."

Scrunching up my face, I shrug my shoulders and wag my head back and forth. "I think we both know that a text can be faked. What time was the body discovered?"

"We got the call around 9:00 a.m."

"That doesn't make sense."

Erick tilts his head and leans forward. "What do you mean?"

"The temperature would've been on the rise

with the sun, I'm assuming. I mean, I'm no meteo-rologist, but it does warm up when the sun comes out, right?"

"True. If Quade was alive at 5:30, he'd have been hard-pressed to freeze in the space of three and a half hours, or less."

"This is what I'm saying." I nod and munch on my fries.

"I agree. Something doesn't add up. We're bringing his partner in for questioning."

"Partner? I thought he was divorced. Is he in a new relationship? A nontraditional one?"

Erick shakes his head. "No. No. Not that kind of partner. This is a business partner. Oscar Wig-gins. They own the dairy together. They're both ar-tisan cheesemakers."

The hairs on the back of my neck tingle. There's something familiar about the name. Without thinking, I close my eyes and sink into a quick psychic replay of the previous two days. "That's where I saw it!"

Erick spills a little of his cocoa and dabs a napkin on his uniform. "What the heck, Moon?"

"Sorry. The name seemed familiar. Oscar Wig-gins attends First Methodist Church."

He dips the edge of his napkin into his water glass and attempts to remove the remainder of the hot chocolate stain from his shirt. "And your point?"

"I don't have one yet. But I knew I'd heard the name before."

He lifts his cup and winks at Tally. "Well, that was totally worth a stain on my uniform."

"I'm sorry, Harper."

Erick smiles and shakes his head. "It's no big deal. If I didn't get one on there by the end of my shift, I'd worry something was wrong in the universe. Something about me and clean shirts, you know? Usually it's coffee, though. That's my go to."

I smile mischievously and lean forward. "Maybe that's why you're so attracted to me? I was one heck of a barista."

He leans across the table, and the heat rolling from his eyes makes my tummy flutter.

Fortunately, Tally arrives with a fresh mug of cocoa and interrupts whatever salacious comment Erick was about to make.

The interruption resets the energy at the table, and we finish our meal without further discussion of murder.

"I gotta get back to the station. I'll let you know if I get any update from the ME, but I don't expect it until late tomorrow—maybe even the day after. If you think of any more fascinating information about Oscar Wiggins, let me know, okay?"

"Ha ha. With that attitude you'll be lucky if I share any of my updates."

He chuckles, slides out of the booth, and kisses me squarely on my unprepared mouth before exiting the diner.

I can't resist a little peek over my shoulder. Leaning out of the booth, I watch my favorite exit. That man can leave anytime he wants. As long as he comes back, of course.

As I turn to situate myself in the booth, I catch sight of Odell shaking his head and chuckling through the red-Formica-trimmed orders-up window. My cheeks flush and I quickly raise a hand to shield my face from further mockery.

It might be time for me to pay Quince Knudsen a visit. I need to find out a bit more about the deceased's ex-wife and the current cheese partner. Before I set up my murder wall, I want to make sure I have a better understanding of how things interconnect.

CHAPTER 7

FIRING OFF a quick text to Quince rewards me with information that the *Pin Cherry Harbor Post* is closed for the week. The elder Knudsen is attending to his brother's estate, and Quince would prefer to meet at the bookstore. We set up a time, and I bundle up appropriately before exiting Myrtle's Diner to brave the Arctic winds whipping across the ice-locked great lake.

My previous experiences with Quince revealed his discomfort around the opposite sex. This tidbit leads me to believe that meeting in the back room on the first floor is preferable to inviting him upstairs to my apartment.

While I wait for him to arrive, I brew up a couple of instant hot chocolates and drop in some mini marshmallows.

A tentative knock on the metal alleyway door announces the arrival of my visitor.

I've seen neither shimmer nor shake of Ghostma, but I fire off a quick telepathic message instructing her to keep her distance just in case she's hovering outside the visual plane.

"Come on in, Quince. I made some cocoa."

A beat-up Chevy truck with rusted-out wheel wells sits in the alley as though abandoned. He rubs his hands together, shivers, and scoots past me to the back room.

"Is that your truck?"

"Yah."

Oh goody, my favorite game. Coax the words from the man-child. "Hey, I'm really sorry about your Uncle Quade. Erick is cooperating, so I'll have more information to work with, and I'll be able to eavesdrop on some interviews tomorrow. For now, it would help to get a better understanding of your uncle's life. Details about the ex-wife, and if you know anything about the dairy and his partner—Oscar Wiggins—that would also be great."

He looks at me as though English isn't his first language, and I sense him struggling mightily to find the courage to share what he knows.

"Look, Quince, I know chatting isn't your thing, but think of it as an important journalistic story. If I don't know the what, why, where, and when, I'm never going to be able to figure out *who* murdered your uncle. So I'm gonna ask you to put on your big-boy pants, and tell me everything."

He nods, takes a swig of hot chocolate, and wipes his mouth with the back of his hand. "K."

I hope that isn't him at his most verbose.

"Like I told you. My uncle is real particular, you know?"

I nod.

"Like, it's kind of a disease. It's why his wife left, you know what I mean?"

Once again, I opt for a physical head nod, rather than risk interrupting his flow with my own verbal response.

"They had a kid. She made my uncle's problems sound pretty bad to the judge, so she got sole custody—no visitation. The whole reason my uncle works so hard at the dairy . . . He's trying to win the kid back over."

"How old is the child?" I couldn't resist. A kettle can only be kept from boiling for so long once the heat is on.

"Oh, he's like fifteen. My uncle was old. Like almost forty or something."

My eyes widen and I stifle a scoff. I remember when I used to think the late thirties were old. As I creep toward my mid-twenties, I'm starting to take a different view of my approaching thirties. "Got it."

"So he took on a partner, to, like, make the dairy more successful."

"Enter Oscar Wiggins. Are they equal partners?"

"My uncle had fifty-one percent share. My dad told him to do that."

"Interesting. Have you ever met your cousin?"

Quince shrugs. "Maybe once, before the divorce."

I completely understand family drama. When my mother discovered she was pregnant and chose to keep me—but not track down the potential father—her parents disowned her. In fact, they couldn't even be bothered to make their way across the pond for her funeral. It's something I haven't forgiven them for, and I'm not sure I ever will. I don't know if I would've enjoyed being raised in England, but I have to think it would've been better than spending over six years in a badly broken foster system.

"Thanks. I know it's not easy to dig through all that family stuff. I'll see if I can sit in on the Oscar Wiggins interview tomorrow. Maybe that will give me a better idea of what they had planned for the dairy, and if those plans created any enemies."

Quince swirls the marshmallows in his cup and replies softly. "Thanks, dude."

He's not pushing his chair back and running for the door, so I lean into my extrasensory perception.

My clairsentience detects a need to be around people. A surprising sensation to receive from Quince.
He prides himself on being a lone wolf.

"Would you like to meet my cat?" Lame. I'm
honestly not great in the entertaining department.

He looks up, shrugs, and nods. "Sure."

Leading the way to the wrought-iron circular
staircase, I offer my standard thirty seconds warning, as I unhook the chain.

He hustles up to the top of the spiral, and I con-
nect the hook behind me.

When I reach the top of the stairway, I call out
to my furry overlord. "Oh, Pyewacket? Pye, there's
someone I'd like you to meet."

Quince glances toward me as though I may be a
tad crazy.

"Don't look at me like that. For a caracal, he
seems to have a fairly decent understanding of
human speech."

My guest shrugs and wanders down one of the
great, curved arms of the mezzanine. His fingers
trace the spines and he's entranced. Glancing back
toward me, he asks, "May I?"

I'm not sure which title he's looking at, but I'm
worried I could draw Twiggy's wrath if I let him
touch a valuable tome with his bare hands. I grab a
pair of white gloves from the nearest oak reading

table and stride toward him. "I'm not sure, but I think you're supposed to wear these. And lay the book down on one of the tables. Don't hold it by the spine."

He slips on the gloves and gently removes the book from the shelf. "Understood."

While he takes the 1646 edition of *Ars Magna Lucis et Umbrae* to a table, I wander the loft in search of the tan terror. As I pass down the opposite arm of the mezzanine, a book rockets out of the shelves, narrowly missing my head.

"Robin Pyewacket Goodfellow! You could've killed me. Stop being a spoiled brat and get down here to meet my friend."

Quince is seated at one of the reading tables, and the green-glass shaded lamp illuminates his selection. It also casts light upon his smirk. Apparently, it amuses him greatly that I speak to my fur baby as though it's human.

Pye saunters toward the interloper, while I retrieve the book from the floor.

Sure enough, it's that same cheesemaking text he was curled up next to earlier. "You can stop hurling books at me, Pye. I've made a note of the title and I will officially log it into evidence."

This comment definitely catches Quince's attention. "So the cat is a snoop too?"

Sighing, I place a hand on my hip. "Rude. I

think the word you're searching for is *sleuth*. And yes, he occasionally helps me on cases."

"Reeeee-ow." A warning.

"Duly noted, master. To be fair, he helps on all my cases."

Quince gazes down at the proud feline. "Cool."

Without further provocation, Pyewacket strides forward and aggressively rubs himself against Quince's leg.

"It would appear that he approves of your praise."

A tender smile erases years from the young man's face. I can almost imagine him as a child, frolicking with a family pet.

He carefully stretches his hand toward Pyewacket. The unpredictable feline takes a hesitant whiff and then licks the outstretched hand with his rough tongue.

Quince chuckles, and risks scratching the beast between the ears.

I swear there's a sound very much like purring coming from the high and mighty Pye.

As I walk away from the recently shelved book, my mood ring burns with a vengeance. I gasp and glance down at the swirling mist inside the smoky black cabochon. The image feels like déjà vu. It's the cover of the book that nearly beaned me: *Mastering Artisan Cheesemaking*.

Throwing my hands in the air, I admit defeat, return to the shelf, and grab the book.

While Quince and Pyewacket are enjoying a mutual admiration society, I plunk into a chair at the nearest reading table and bone up on the art of cheesemaking. Not much of what I'm perusing makes sense, but I feel as though I'm cramming for an exam. Phrases like traditional rennet, direct acidification, and recombinant bacteria flow into my brain to possibly be forever ignored. However, one of those strange phrases could come in handy tomorrow when I drop into the sheriff's station to evaluate Oscar Wiggins.

Pye has taken up residence on the table next to Quince's right arm, and the young man is diligently studying the engravings amongst the ancient text while he absently strokes the feline.

Somehow the day has gotten the better of me and my eyelids seem to be made of lead. "Hey, I think I'm gonna crash out. You're welcome to come back tomorrow if you'd like to keep looking at that book. Just leave it on the table with the gloves and I'll leave a note for Twiggy. That way, if she has a problem with it, she can take it out on me."

He chuckles, sits back, and removes the gloves. "Cool."

I walk down to the back door with him, lock up, and set the alarm. As I march toward my swanky apartment, I call out to Grams and the entitled feline. "It sure would be nice if one of you would hand over a clue about the missing baby Jesus! In case you've forgotten, I have two cases to solve now. Three if we're counting that infernal coat!"

Pyewacket ignores me, and Grams remains cloaked from my otherworldly receptors.

CHAPTER 8

THE BLEAK WINTER sun barely has the strength to penetrate my slumped-glass windows, and offers no warmth or promise of spring. As a resident of the Southwest, I'd heard rumors about something called seasonal affective disorder. I could never imagine such a thing. Most folks in Arizona would give a week's pay for a break from the relentless desert sun. However, now that I reside in almost-Canada, I long for a day filled with azure skies, dense cotton-ball clouds, and heat that penetrates to the bone.

For now, I'll have to settle for the warmth of my reindeer onesie pajamas and a thick flannel-lined bathrobe.

Stumbling downstairs, I pry open one eye far enough to brew a passable cup of coffee and pour a glug of questionable half-and-half into my cup.

Still no sign of my ghostly grandmother.

Time to hike up to the third floor of the printing museum.

Pushing the bar on the door and scraping across the finished concrete floor activates some strange level of hyper-hearing, which I've never experienced. The hairs on the back of my neck stand on end and there are murmuring voices.

Plural.

Even though I'm only half awake, I spin and grab the door leading back to the bookshop before it can slam. I ride it home as silently as possible and creep toward the base of the staircase. The usual comfort I feel in this part of the building evaporates as something in my psychic toolkit strains to identify the sounds.

I wish I could say I've gone up and down the stairs enough times to remember every spot that creaks, but it's simply not true. Another movie trope shattered. Most of the time I'm either in a ridiculous rush, or I'm having some sort of argument with Ghost-ma.

This trip takes on a new and spine-tingling twist as I struggle for silence.

When I reach the landing on the second floor, I'm forced to stop and re-evaluate my plan.

Or should I say, my complete lack of a plan?

I'm wearing pajamas, a robe, and I'm holding a

hot cup of coffee. Not exactly what one would call "ninja gear."

What are they doing in this museum? Suddenly, it occurs to me that many of the artifacts are probably more valuable than I imagine, and it wouldn't be the first time someone has tried to steal something from my place of business.

Now my curiosity transforms into a cold sweat. I should probably call Erick. As I struggle to fish my phone from the pocket of my robe, recognition dawns.

Odell! The other voice is Odell! Grams must be talking as she writes out the messages for him to read.

Now that I've identified the voices as Grams and her first husband, I feel like a peeping Tom who's fallen into the beams of a police cruiser's headlights.

It's completely inappropriate for me to eavesdrop on their private conversation.

Turning to creep back down the stairs and possibly steal some of Pyewacket's Fruity Puffs, my foot catches on the hem of the robe—

Next thing you know, I'm lying at the bottom of a flight of stairs next to a broken coffee mug, and I'm covered in stains of the same.

Odell thunders down the stairs and I call out weakly, "It's me. It was only me. I didn't mean to—"

"Mitzy! What the heck? Are you okay?"

He's at my side in a minute and helps me to a seat on the bottom step.

"What happened, kid?"

He's always been fond of me, but, somehow, now that I know he's my actual grandfather, his concern is warming a whole new part of my heart. "Don't worry. I'm totally fine. I couldn't find Grams . . . There were voices . . . When I figured out it was you . . . My exit was supposed to be stealthy."

His raucous laughter joins my grandmother's near squeal, and I drop my head into my hands. "Thanks, guys. Real vote of confidence."

Odell shakes his head, stands, and offers me a hand. "Here, let me help you up."

I take his outstretched hand and, as I lean forward to get to my feet, a sharp pain shoots through my left ankle. "Ouch!"

He scoops an arm around my waist. "Which ankle?"

"Are you psychic?"

My question catches him completely off guard, and he chokes on his denial.

"No more secrets, remember? Now that we know the truth about my genealogy, it seems like there's a real good chance I didn't inherit all of my gifts from Grams."

Odell looks down and smiles warmly. "Heck, I never thought of it in those terms. I figured I was smarter than the average bear, that's all."

"Oh, come on. You can't kid a kidder, Gramps."

He shakes his head and runs his free hand through his buzz cut nervously. "Maybe there's somethin' to what you're saying. I never thought much about it."

Ghost-ma swirls closer and chill bumps rise on Odell's exposed forearms.

His initial shock from discovering the existence of Isadora's ghost has been replaced with soul-bonding comfort. He glances at his arms and smiles broadly. "Whaddya think, Myrtle? Maybe I got one or two gifts too, eh?"

Grams giggles like a schoolgirl. "Tell him I think he's got all the gifts, sweetie."

Rolling my eyes, I look up at Odell and grin. "I'm really not interested in being an afterlife love-letter interpreter, so I'll just say Grams thinks you're the bee's knees and we'll leave it at that."

He chuckles. "We can debate the finer points of the family tree later. I'm taking you to the hospital. If it ain't broke, it's definitely a bad sprain."

Moaning with the gusto of a spoiled child, I slip my arm around Odell's neck and hop up onto my right foot. "All right, but you have to let me change. I'm not going to the hospital in reindeer onesie PJs."

He smiles and winks. "Aw, don't worry. You look cute as a button."

Punching him playfully in the side, I continue my protest. "It's not the cute factor that concerns me. I've seen all the hospital dramas on television. As soon as I get in there, they're going to take a pair of surgical scissors and cut these adorable pajamas right off me. These PJs are one of the few things I brought from Arizona, and I don't want to see 'em destroyed by an overzealous intern."

Both my grandparents chuckle at my protest, and Odell consents to help me up to the apartment and wait outside while I clumsily get changed.

Luckily, Grams joins me in the apartment and attempts to offer as much assistance as her semi-corporeal form will allow.

At long last, I work my way into a pair of flair-legged yoga pants, and top them off with a T-shirt sporting a huge fake bloodstain on the right side and the simple phrase, "I'M FINE," across the chest.

Grams protests, but I insist the joke will absolutely land with the audience in Emergency.

Her eyes roll as she floats to the exit and summons enough physicality to push the twisted ivy medallion inside the apartment that activates the sliding bookcase door.

Odell stands just outside the entrance with his back turned. "Are you decent?"

"Depends who you ask?"

He spins around and chokes when he sees my shirt. "You are one-of-a-kind, Mitzy Moon. One-of-a-kind."

I clumsily take a hopping, one-legged bow, and he hurries to my side to escort me down to my new Jeep. En route to the hospital, I attempt to convince him to park and allow me to walk in, but he pulls the "grandpa card" and insists on driving up to the emergency entrance.

An orderly bustles out with a wheelchair, and I glare at Odell. "I'm going to remember this, Mr. Johnson."

He laughs too easily. "I'll park this thing and meet you inside. And don't break your other foot while you're waiting."

"Rude."

After explaining it's an ankle sprain and not a gunshot wound, as the humor of my T-shirt implies, the orderly wheels me inside and the nurse behind the desk smiles with recognition when I give her my name. "Oh, I've read about you in the paper. Were you working on a case when you injured yourself, Miss Moon?"

I'm tempted to offer a simple white lie, but the true story of my injury will bring far more laughs when she retells it in the break room. "I wish. Sadly, I was simply walking down the stairs at the printing museum, and caught my foot on the hem of my robe." I shrug and shake my head. "Just your standard variety klutz."

She leans forward and winks. "Gotcha. Your secret's safe with me. I figure you're working on the case of the missing baby Jesus and don't want to tip off Mrs. Coleman."

I didn't see that coming. Clearly, my attempt to tell the truth and not exaggerate my exploits turned into a supposed conspiracy. Wow! I can't imagine how frustrating it must be for the actually famous. I assume people make up stories and take creative license with celebrities' stories all the time. Another reason to enjoy small-town living.

Hold on, did she say, "Tip off Mrs. Coleman"? That warrants a follow-up question. "To be honest, I'm looking into that, but Mrs. Coleman was quite helpful."

The woman rolls her eyes extravagantly and scoffs. "Oh, honey, don't fall for it. She caught one whiff of the proposed Nativity 'upgrade' and she did not turn the other cheek. Apparently, her great-great-something or other gifted that set to the church. Well, you didn't hear it from me, but I wouldn't put it past her to tuck that infant savior in her own trunk to throw a wrench in the plans." She widens her eyes, lifts her brows, and shakes her head as she "Mm-mm-ms" under her breath.

The silence hangs awkwardly between us, and it's my turn. I lean toward the glass partition and whisper through the hole, "Thanks for the tip." Winking as the orderly wheels me away, she rewards me with a matching conspiratorial smile.

After x-rays and a physical examination—which proves more painful than my actual fall—the doctor shares my diagnosis.

"Miss Moon, you're suffering from a Grade 1 anatomical sprain and a mild concussion. I recommend the RICE protocol: Rest, Ice, Compression, and Elevation. You'll have to wear a Velcro boot for one to two weeks, and use a single crutch to keep the weight off the ankle. Do you understand?"

"Yes, ma'am." I feel like a kid in the principal's office getting assigned detention. This doctor's bedside manner could do with a "warm up." For the record, she was not amused by my graphic tee. Guess I wildly misread the room on that one.

She clears her throat and pinches her lips together. "As for the concussion, it's likely a Grade 2. Mild but requiring rest. Avoid operating a motor vehicle for at least forty-eight hours."

"Yes, ma'am." If I didn't live within hobbling distance of everything that mattered to me, I might put up a fuss. However, I'll still be able to make it to the diner and the sheriff's station. Sure, it'll take me three times as long, but at least I won't miss any important suspect interviews.

The doctor exits without any pleasantries, and a nurse enters with paperwork.

After signing myself out and taking my aftercare instructions, Odell picks up my prescription painkillers and drives me back to the bookshop to make sure I tell Grams about the precautions I'm supposed to be taking.

"She may not be able to stop you, but, if I know Myrtle, she'll find a way to make you do as you were told."

Lifting my eyebrows, I nod in agreement. "Oh, you don't know the half of it."

After handing me a pain pill, and making sure I drink the entire glass of water, Odell sets the medication in my bathroom. "It's on the counter," he says as he situates me on the settee, elevates my injured leg, and places the hospital-issue ice pack on my left ankle. "If you need anything, just call the diner. I can be here in five minutes or less."

"Thanks, Gramps."

He shakes his head and chuckles as he leaves.

Pyewacket creeps across the thick carpet as though he's stalking prey. He circles the contraption on my foot and lifts his nose in the air to see if the smell is one that should concern him.

"Don't worry. It's only a little walking boot to

protect my sprained ankle. Not all of us are blessed with your reflexes, Pyewacket. Or your endless supply of lives!"

"Ree-ow." Soft but condescending.

Satisfied with my explanation, the spoiled caracal saunters off to find his own entertainment.

The trip to the hospital, the tests, exams, and endless waiting chewed up most of my day. I hope I didn't miss the dairy partner interrogation.

Only one way to find out . . .

Time for me to update my boyfriend.

Would it surprise you to hear that Erick is not shocked by my report? In fact, he honestly can't believe I wasn't more seriously injured. He offers to come and pick me up for the Oscar Wiggins interview, but I insist I'm a self-sufficient, independent woman and will make my own way to the station.

The psychic in me warns that I'll regret that assumption.

CHAPTER 9

You know what? Being a self-sufficient, independent woman isn't all it's cracked up to be. As I crutch my way down Main Street, I'm out of breath and my ankle is throbbing. Maybe I should've taken two pain pills. It seems far colder outside than I remember, and the patches of un-shoveled sidewalk make my hop more dangerous than I'd hoped.

While I struggle to coordinate door, crutch, walking boot, and not falling over—

"Moon! I can't believe you wouldn't let me help you." Erick takes my crutch, slips his arm around my waist, and practically carries me to the observation room.

I would never admit it out loud, but he really is my knight in shining armor. I can be a modern woman and still accept a gallant gesture from Sheriff Too-Hot-To-Handle. "Thank you, kind sir."

"Not a problem, m'lady."

"I'll wait here for you, Sheriff."

He grins, kisses the top of my head, and walks out of the observation room.

From my perch in the glass-encased spy nook, I glean what I can from the interview subject's demeanor before the sheriff enters.

Oscar Wiggins sits calmly in Interrogation Room 2. His shoulders are broad and his strong hands show the scars of manual labor, but his vibe is more metro-sexual hipster than redneck farmer. He removes a miniature comb from his plaid shirt pocket and grooms his meticulously trimmed mustache. He slips it back into the pocket and admires his reflection. Not a single dark-brown hair on his face, or head, dares to be out of place.

I'm not picking up anything disconcerting through the one-way glass. That's a good sign. Although not helpful as far as suspects go.

I brilliantly use the tip of my crutch to flip the silver toggle switch, and Erick's in-charge work voice flows through the speaker.

"Now that we've got the particulars out of the way, thank you for coming in today, Mr. Wiggins. I understand you and the deceased were partners in the dairy. How long had you and Mr. Knudsen been in business together?"

Good job, Erick. Start him out with a softball question and loosen his tongue.

"I'm happy to assist in the investigation, Sheriff. Quade wasn't just a business partner, he was a good friend. Me and the wife used to have him over for supper at least once a week. It was tough for him, you know? Being all alone and everything."

Erick nods. "And how long had you been in business together?"

"Oh, right. What happened was, I worked for a big dairy down south, and the commute was killing me. I offered to do some consulting for Quade, and we just hit it off, you know?" He strokes his close-clipped goatee and nods.

A woman doesn't need clairsentience to pick up on Erick's frustration with the unanswered question. Hopefully third time's a charm.

"And when did you start this consulting?"

"Well, let's see." Oscar presses his thumb against his lower lip. "Seems like that was almost six years ago. Boy, time flies."

Erick makes a couple of notes in his pad and continues. "And when did you sign the partnership agreement?"

Oscar angles away and places both of his thick hands on the edge of the table—rhythmically strumming his fingers as he ponders the question. "Gee, I think I did the consulting for about a year, then I came on full-time at Quade's dairy. That maybe only lasted six or eight months, and— Well, he was in a bit of financial trouble. He was going to take out a big loan, but I suggested the partnership as a way to keep things afloat and avoid more debt."

"So would you say the partnership agreement was signed roughly four years ago?"

Erick is quickly losing patience with this attention-deficient interviewee.

"What? Oh, yes. Four years. Mmhmm. Sounds right." Oscar seems distracted by his own image in the one-way glass.

"And were you able to turn the dairy around? Was it profitable?"

Mr. Wiggins nods several times, but then he shakes his head and shrugs. "It was doing all right. Not necessarily turning a profit. We had plans to change all that. We were going to hammer out an agreement to sub-produce for one of the big dairies down south. It was going to put us on the fast track to success, you know?"

Erick scribbles in his notepad, and silence hangs in the air. I can sense Oscar's discomfort, but most people are uneasy when being questioned by law enforcement.

The sheriff stops writing and tilts his head.

"This sub-producing contract was your idea, or Quade's?"

Oscar shrugs and shakes his head in confusion. "I can't be sure who thought of it. We had a lot of long conversations over bourbon, after those weekly dinners."

Bourbon? Maybe Quince doesn't know his uncle as well as he thinks.

"Anyone else know about these conversations?" Erick taps his pen once.

"Tammy might remember, but as far as I know it just came up."

"And Tammy is your wife?"

The man laughs uncomfortably. "She sure is. And won't let me forget it for a minute. You know how the old ball and chain can be."

I angle my body forward and reach out with all my psychic senses. I can't wait to see how Erick answers that question.

"Can't say that I do, Mr. Wiggins. But I've heard the sentiment before. I'll make a note to ask Tammy about that line item. Is this sub-producer contract moving forward?"

Oscar takes a deep breath and schools his features carefully. There's a hint of excitement beneath his somber, well-groomed exterior. "Yeah, it's a real shame Quade won't be around to reap the rewards. But I feel good knowing it was his dying wish."

In case you're wondering, I'm not the only one who isn't buying that performance.

Erick crosses his arms and inhales—real slow. "His dying wish? Are you saying that this conversation about the sub-producing was the last thing you and Quade spoke about?"

Oscar swallows and shakes his head. "Well, no. I didn't mean it like that. It was just a stupid expression. Sorry, I'm a little shook up by all of this. Poor choice of words, Sheriff. I don't remember the last thing we spoke about. Probably something mundane, like cleaning the milking equipment or ordering more feed."

Erick nods, but makes a lengthy note in his pad.

"That'll be all for now, Mr. Wiggins. I'll speak to your wife about the contract conversation, and we'll be in touch if we need any additional information from you."

Oscar nods and hesitantly gets to his feet. "Is it all right if I leave, Sheriff?"

"You're free to go. But don't leave town just yet."

Mr. Wiggins' spine stiffens, and he hustles out of the interrogation room.

Rather than rushing out of the observation room to sit innocently in Erick's office, I feel as though I have permission to sit comfortably and wait for him to check in. My grown-up patience pays off as he peeks into the room.

"Any hunches?" He tilts his head hopefully.

"Not at present. Although, I'm curious to see if Tammy can fill in some details on that sub-producing tidbit." I reach for my crutch, but my thoughtful boyfriend beats me to the punch.

"There's no crime in asking for help, Moon." His tone is scolding, but he offers me one hand and holds the crutch in his other.

I smile and accept his assistance. "Unless you're asking for help to commit murder."

The comment hits him square in the gut and he exhales sharply before laughing. "Nice way to put it in perspective." He places the crutch under my left arm and holds my right hand until I'm situated.

Smiling up at him, with what I hope are feminine wiles, I ask, "In the interest of accepting help, could I possibly get a police escort back to the bookshop?"

He nods and purposefully chews the inside of his cheek. "Of course. Let me see if Paulsen is available." Erick turns, and I let out a little squeak of protest. He spins back with a smug grin on his face. "Gotcha."

"Good one, Harper. You definitely got me."

Graciously assisting me into the hallway, he

grabs a winter jacket from his office. "Deputy Baird, I'm headed—out for the night. Call me if you need me."

She frowns knowingly. "10-4, Sheriff."

I purposely avoid making eye contact with the perceptive deputy. My quick-to-blush cheeks will certainly confirm any suspicions she might have about exactly where Erick is headed.

Walking back toward the bookshop, just the two of us, reminds me of the first time we held hands. The thrill that raced up my arm that day hasn't lessened a bit. In fact, each day I spend with him makes me more and more sure that this is the path I'm supposed to be on.

I don't want to tempt fate by making too many plans for the future. I'm just going to hobble through the snow with this wonderful man's arm around my waist, and be grateful for all the treasures I've uncovered in almost-Canada.

Erick insists on unhooking the chain at the bottom of the spiral staircase, despite my Twiggy-related protests. He's far too acquainted with accident-prone Mitzy to back down. In the end, we make it past and get the chain re-secured within the thirty-second window.

Hopefully banishing Grams from the apartment for the evening will go as smoothly.

As if on cue—

"I'm happy to give you and Erick some privacy, dear. All you have to do is ask nicely. You'd be surprised how cooperative people can be. More flies with honey, I always say."

As Erick reaches up to pull the candle handle, I clear my throat and mumble, "I have to take care of a little family business, Erick."

He turns hesitantly and searches the air around me. "Isadora?"

"The one and only." Navigating a slow crutch-supported turn, I address the ghost. "Grams, Erick was kind enough to walk me home and we're probably going to order some food and hang out. Would you please give us some privacy?"

Ghost-ma twists one of her diamond rings and adjusts a strand of pearls. "Now, that wasn't so hard, was it?"

Not willing to let her get in the last word, I send her a brief telepathic message. *You better hightail it to the printing museum, Missy, or there's going to be some hot couture, and that's H-O-T!*

Her face is a glowing mask of horror as she vanishes through the wall into the museum.

Threatening to start her vintage fashion on fire is always a power move.

"Are we clear?" Erick searches the air a second time and his eyes grow wide.

"All clear."

He helps me to the over-stuffed settee, and once I'm safely in a seated position, gently pulls off my coat.

Taking advantage of his nearness, I secretly inhale his citrus-woodsy scent.

Laying the coat over the back of the sofa, he asks, "I heard some mention of ordering food. Were you serious?"

Rubbing my hands together in anticipation, I grin. "I'm hoping. Do you think Dante might be working at Angelo and Vinci's? I'm happy to pay a delivery charge if he's willing to run over."

Erick smiles. "Nice. Now you're thinking like a local, and an heiress."

"You're not wrong." Rather than be offended, I take it as a compliment. I honestly don't mind spreading a little goodwill. The Duncan-Moon coffers can certainly cover a couple generous portions of the world's best lasagna!

Once the important business of ordering sustenance has been handled, and Dante has been promised a hefty tip, Erick throws out a suggestion. "Do you want to play a board game?"

I choke on my reply, and it takes several seconds for me to regroup and respond. "A board game? Look, Harper, I'm not going to pretend to be a relationship expert, but I don't want to move to the board game phase for at least a few more months."

He blushes adorably. "Yeah, it sounded wrong as soon as it came out of my mouth. It's just that you're kinda injured and I don't want to make things worse."

Perhaps I shouldn't, but it's so much fun to make him uncomfortable. "Make things worse? How do you mean?" Oh, that color of red looks so good on his cheeks.

"Well, you know— I was thinking—"

"Let me put you out of your misery, Sheriff. Why don't we start with supper and see where the night takes us?"

He swallows audibly. "Yeah, your plan is better."

CHAPTER 10

WHEN HARSH WINTER light stabs its early morning fingers into my eyes, my first instinct is to scold myself. What an idiot! I can't believe I forgot to close the blackout blinds before I went to bed.

Thankfully, those thoughts are kept on the inside of my head, and they are quickly replaced by a wash of warm, tingly memories.

Oh, that's right. Last night, when yummy Erick Harper was kissing the side of my neck, the last thing on my mind was window shades or morning.

Carefully turning beneath the thick down comforter, I risk a peek at my sleepover guest.

Erick, who grew up in Pin Cherry, must be more accustomed to the frosty temperatures. Sometime during the night, he got too hot—no pun intended; I swear—and pushed the comforter down, exposing his lovely washboard abs for inspection. Plus, his tousled, soft blond hair is begging me to run my fingers through it.

Exercising all the self-control I don't possess, I keep my hands to myself and enjoy the view for a moment longer.

Before I finish soaking it all in, one sleepy eyelid cracks open and a mischievous bright-blue eye locks onto me like a laser-targeting system. "Whatever you're planning over there, Moon, it will have to wait."

Struggling to swallow, I jump to my defense. "Planning? I wasn't planning anything. I was—"

He rolls onto his side and props up his mussed head of hair on one rippling bicep. "Mmhmm, go on. I'm gonna go ahead and let you try to finish that sentence."

A blush of heat creeps up my cheeks and I've never been so thankful for a caracal interruption.

Pyewacket lands with a thud between us and offers a warning thwack to my left shoulder.

"Message received, my furry overlord." I twist and groan and drag myself out of the heavenly co-coon. "I gotta pour some Fruity Puffs for Pye, but I'll be back to discuss whatever it is you think you know."

He sits up, stretches his arms wide, and tries to

speak as he yawns. "No hurry. I can watch you walk away all day."

I tug down the bottom of my sleeping T-shirt and giggle. "Hey, that's my line."

His hoarse chuckle echoes down the stairs as I limp toward the back room to fix a heaping bowl of sugary children's cereal for my entitled feline.

"I gave you an extra-large portion, because you were such a good kitty last night. Thank you for respecting my privacy." I nearly make the mistake of ending my praise by scratching his head between his black-tufted ears, but that's a mistake you only make once. Never interrupt a caracal when he's eating.

No sign of Grams—which is excellent.

I hobble upstairs, trying my best to keep the weight off my left foot, even though I forgot my crutch somewhere in the apartment.

Shambling back into the cozy room with high hopes, I'm disappointed to discover my drowsy boyfriend is no longer lounging on my antique four-poster. He's dressed and ready for action. "You're leaving? Already?"

Erick strides across the room in a slightly crumpled tan uniform, scoops me into his arms, and kisses me deliciously. "Some of us have to work for a living."

"Oh brother! I have a job. I'm looking into the

disappearance of the miniature Messiah from a certain local Nativity set."

His easy grin disappears, and his sheriff's voice joins the party. "Look, Moon, I want you to take it easy on that ankle. Sprains can take longer to heal than breaks. Don't push your luck. And if I know you, you're always pushing your luck. So act like a real heiress for one day. Sit on your sofa, eat bonbons, and watch old movies. I'll check on you at lunchtime."

He offers my cheek one last gentle kiss and walks toward the spiral staircase.

Yes, I do watch him leave. However, I don't let him get away without a fight. "I have never eaten bonbons in my life, Sheriff Harper!"

He laughs all the way out the alley door.

With all the ankle spraining shenanigans and everyone insisting that I take it easy, I nearly forgot about the curious case of Mrs. Coleman. However, today I'm unsupervised and I think it's time to grab my keys and take a little convalescence drive.

As I pick up my dealership-issue keychain, I fully expect Grams to burst through the floor or the wall and admonish me, but the apartment is silent. Twenty-four hours is almost forty-eight, right?

It's my lucky day.

The yoga pants I previously eased over my injured foot can certainly pass for one more day, and the T-shirt I slept in is barely even wrinkled. Plus, the message will serve as my mantra for the day. "Curiosity killed the cat, but satisfaction brought him back!" There's an image of a smug feline perched next to the idiom.

Managing the crutch, the circular stairs, and the "No Admittance" chain proves a tall order for my inborn clumsiness. So I breathe a heavy sigh of relief when I make it safely to the first floor, and get the chain hooked back in place without setting off the alarm.

Things are going swimmingly.

"And where do you think you're going, young lady?"

Spoke too soon.

Grams rockets toward me in a mini ghost-rage. "Keys? Why on earth do you have keys? You're not supposed to drive for at least two days!"

"Simmer down, Isadora. It's my left foot that's injured. All the driving stuff happens with the right foot. It's not like I have a manual transmission. Who even knows what that is anymore?"

She crosses her arms and strums her perfectly manicured fingers on the burgundy silk-and-tulle. "I don't know, dear. The foot isn't the issue. According to Odell, it's the concussion we're supposed to worry about. Plus, it all seems too dangerous. I don't like the idea of you poking around, looking for a potential murderer in your condition."

My jaw falls open like Old Mother Hubbard's cupboard. "My condition! It's not like I'm pregnant. It's a little ankle sprain. It's nothing."

Salty tears build up in the corner of Ghost-ma's eyes. "Just the thought of a great grandbaby . . ."

"Do not start with me. We've had this discussion, and we are not having it again. And it's not like I'm looking around for a killer. I'm not insane."

"But you have to find out who killed Quince's uncle?"

"All in due time. Right now, I'm simply following up on a missing Messiah lead. There'll be time to sweep up potential murderers after I've put things right in the Nativity scene."

Grams reaches an ethereal hand toward me and pats my shoulder. "You're a good egg, Mitzy. I'd be proud of you even if you weren't my granddaughter."

Grabbing the handle on the alleyway door, I can't keep the thought from popping into my head: *But it doesn't hurt that I'm an egg from your farm.*

"Well, I never—"

As I let the door slam closed, I spout my favorite refrain. "Oh, we all know different, Myrtle Isadora Johnson Linder Duncan Willamet Rogers."

Not for the first time, I'm pleased that the ghost

of my dear grandmother is tethered to the bookshop and can't follow me down the alleyway to continue her defense.

The parking lot at the First Methodist Church is freshly plowed, and the man-made snowdrifts at the back of the lot tower above my Jeep. They're also an unattractive muddy brown with streaks of black. I can't wait for the weather to turn, and all of this snowdrift nonsense to melt away.

Despite the exposed pavement, I take it real slow as I approach the sanctuary. Once inside, I tug off my beanie and shove it in the pocket of my puffy coat.

Mrs. Coleman's door stands open as I approach. The noxious potpourri has leaked into the hallway. I grab one last breath of fresh-ish air and crutch on in.

"Good morning, Mrs. Coleman. Do you have a minute?"

She beams warmly, teeth and all, and gestures to a thinly padded seat in her spacious quarters.

I lower myself onto the ruffled gingham as my gaze clocks the plethora of porcelain cats perched on every flat surface. How did I miss that last time?

"Did you find our Lord and Savior?"

That opening line reminds me of a very different discussion I had with foster family number three. "I think I'm closing in on Him. I've gotten some good leads. Which is why I'm here. Rumor has it the Nativity scene was scheduled for a makeover."

Her baleful gasp interrupts my report. "Folks just don't appreciate history anymore."

"I couldn't agree more. Was there anyone specifically opposed to the refresh?"

Her beady eyes dart left and right, as though seeking the support of her feline army. "There were congregants on both sides of the argument."

That tells me what I need to know about her. Old guard—definitely. Now, to define the new guard. "So, who was pushing for the change?"

"There were three or four ladies who were particularly adamant. Just didn't appreciate the nostalgia of the set we have. I said I wasn't against some thoughtful restoration, but throwing the whole thing, and the gift it represents, out the door . . . I said it seemed unchristian."

Whew! That comment must've ruffled some feathers, but I'll keep that side note to myself. "What's the status of the project now that the baby Jesus has gone missing?"

She shuffles some papers on her desk, pulls her lips together over her chompers, and sniffles loudly. "They're pushing forward vigorously. They claim it wouldn't be right to replace part of the set and not the rest. Even said something about favoritism or design flaws . . . It's all a blur, really. I just find the thefts upsetting."

"Thefts? Are you talking about the list?"

Mrs. Coleman tilts her head in confusion, but a moment later her lips curl into a wan smile revealing "all she wants for Christmas." "Oh my goodness! I forgot to tell you. I placed that list in the file with the copy for this week's bulletin. When I pulled out the folder to start the copies, there was the attendance list. So, there was only the one theft. I'm not sure what I was thinking when I placed it in there. The list is safe. Just the kidnapping of our sweet baby from the manger." She dabs at a nonexistent tear.

"Has there been a ransom demand?"

Her close-set eyes widen, and her mouth slowly forms a perfect O, but no sound comes out.

"I didn't mean to upset you, Mrs. Coleman. I thought maybe if it was more than a prank, there might have been some monetary motivation."

She shakes her head vigorously. "There's been no such demand. And if the pastor had gotten such a call, I certainly would know about it. Why just this morning I was saying—"

Before she can tell me what she said, I jump in.

"Could you write down the names of the congregants pushing for the new Nativity?"

The woman nods absently, but her gaze remains fixed on a point in space.

"Mrs. Coleman?"

She looks at me as though I've appeared out of thin air. "Oh, yes dear. Forgive me."

I'd love to make a missing-baby-Jesus quip right now regarding her forgiveness, but taking a moment to read the room . . . this isn't the time or the place.

She scribbles four or five names on a piece of paper, double-checks it, and hands it to me. "I spoke to the reverend about this. I said, 'If someone from our own congregation is behind this . . . Well, how disappointing.'"

I smile and nod as I take the slip of paper from her outstretched hand. "I'll keep looking, Mrs. Coleman. Don't worry."

"Thank you, dear."

And with that, I shove the slip of paper in the pocket of my coat, hobble down the hallway and out the side door.

CHAPTER 11

As I HEAD BACK toward Bell, Book & Candle, I unhappily check something off my list. The attendance list wasn't stolen, which makes it less likely that a congregant is responsible for the theft of the baby Jesus from the manger. Only someone inside the church system would've known about the attendance list, and the connection between that missing roll sheet and the statuette made sense to me, at the time.

Now my suspect pool went from the folks in attendance at the First Methodist Church on a particular Sunday to anyone in Pin Cherry Harbor or the surrounding area.

Grrr. Argh.

Before I can get the alleyway door open wide

enough to stumble through, Grams is already hitting me with a complaint.

However, once I'm safely inside the bookstore, I realize her issue isn't with me at all. For the first time I can remember, she's legitimately upset with Pyewacket.

"You have to do something, Mitzy. That monster is dragging a horrible rag all over the bookstore. He tried to take it up to the apartment, and it took every ounce of strength I had to scare him back down the stairs. Can you imagine if he'd gotten the nasty thing near my couture?!"

"*Your* couture. Hold on a minute, Grams. I distinctly remember the wording in your last will and testament. 'Everything inside the Bell, Book & Candle Bookshop and Printing Museum is to become the sole property of Mizithra Achelois Moon.'"

Her tantrum ends abruptly, and she squeezes her expertly drawn eyebrows together, creating a soft furrow above her nose. "Did you honestly remember that phrase verbatim or are you using your psychic recall?"

The question catches me off guard and I have to let it rattle around in my noggin for a minute or so. "Well, I'm honestly not sure. I think I used my psychic recall. No. I did. I saw the page— I was on the bus—"

She floats toward me and whispers in awe. "Sweetie, you're getting really good. I remember when you used to take several minutes to calm yourself and focus before you could access your gifts. You did that in the middle of an argument! In the blink of an eye!" She claps her hands together gleefully and swirls around me as though she's an entire circle of children playing Ring Around the Rosie.

"Did I? I mean, I actually did."

Pyewacket rises onto his hind legs and rubs the nasty rag against my day-old yoga pants.

Grams chuckles. "I'm not sure you're doing that math correctly, dear. Seems like it's been more than one day." She purses her lips and looks down her nose at my sorely lacking sense of fashion.

"Ignore her, Pyewacket. There must be something very important about this rag." I remove it from his mouth, and he rewards me with a response.

"Reow." Can confirm.

"I'll take it up to the murder wall and officially log it into evidence."

As I spin on my crutch to make my way upstairs, Pyewacket leaps in my way and offers a frightening warning. "Reeeee-ow."

"Easy, big guy. I'm on your side. Remember?" Dangling the filthy rag between my thumb and forefinger, I look at Grams and shrug. "Any ideas?"

She floats backward and shivers with disgust.

"All right, Pye. Help me out here. If you don't want me to take this upstairs, do you want me to give it to Erick?"

He plunks his tan behind down and seems to shake his head in a very human way.

"So that's a 'no' to Erick." Running through my short list of options, I choose my photojournalist friend next. "Is it something I should ask Quince about?"

"Reow." Can confirm.

That's one for team Mitzy. Before I can continue my Twenty Questions with the cat, the word icehouse hits my brain like an invisible mortar round. "Icehouse? Do you want me to go back out to check the icehouse for something?"

"RE-OW!" Game on!

Spinning the keys around my finger, I head toward the back door.

Grams summons all of her otherworldly strength, takes semi-corporeal form, and plants a fist on either hip—directly in my path. "I will haunt your apartment till the end of times! You and that sexy sheriff will never have another moment's peace."

"What's the deal? That's a little harsh."

"You call that Quince Knudsen and tell him to pick you up. I'm not against you continuing your investigation. You know how smart I think you are, dear. But you get the boy to drive you out there and watch your back. You're not at your best, physically. I'd never forgive myself if something happened, sweetie."

"Copy that."

A quick call to Quince confirms that he's as bored as I am, and happy to drive me out to his uncle Quade's ice-fishing house.

The drive out to one of the hundreds of lakes dotting the Birch County countryside seems longer than I remember. Perhaps it's the psychic itch begging to be scratched that makes the journey interminable.

"Did you ever go ice fishing with your uncle?"

Quince shrugs. "Couple times."

"Not your thing?"

He sighs and taps his thumb on the steering wheel. "He really likes to be alone. Like, for real."

I shrug and shiver. "Can you turn the heater up?"

Quince shakes his head and groans softly. "It's kinda busted."

Just the thought of no heater sends my body into a full spasm. "What? How busted is kinda?"

He snickers. "Pretty much totally. That's why

there's duct tape on the windows. Grab those hoodies behind the seat, if you want."

"Dude!" My panic has sent me headfirst into the young man's word pool. "We could freeze to death."

The smile disappears from his face in a flash, and he grips the steering wheel with both hands.

"Oh shoot. Quince, I'm so sorry. My brain just goes into the dark humor anytime I get uncomfortable. I honestly didn't mean to—"

His Adam's apple bobs as he struggles to swallow. "It's cool. No biggie."

It absolutely was a biggie. A monstrous faux pas. Even though it didn't cross my mind at the time, the callous reference to freezing to death clearly seems like an attempt to make light of his uncle's passing. Sadly, I've been in this situation a few too many times before, and I've learned the hard way that the more I talk, the worse I make it for myself. I shiver in silence and take winter's wrath as the penance I deserve.

The next turn sparks something in my memory and a sense of relief floods over me as we draw near the icehouse.

Quince parks and meets me at the edge of the frozen lake. "What are we looking for?"

"I'm not exactly sure, but I'll know it when I see it."

"Do we break the yellow tape?"

"Hold on a minute." Following the crime scene tape around the structure that's barely larger than a port-a-potty, I find the loose end tucked under and carefully pull it free. Unwrapping the "not" present, I instruct Quince to keep his gloves on as I open the door.

"I'll check the outside while you check the inside. There's not really room for both of us in there. If you don't find anything, we'll swap."

He blushes at the mere thought of having to be in such close quarters with me, and I begin my search of the exterior.

It's a simple wooden structure with a small window opposite the door. The roof is slightly pitched and the blue paint peels and curls from the effects of the harsh weather.

Other than the screw we recovered earlier, there are no unusual marks on the exterior of the tiny building. The window is closed tightly, and the snow has drifted halfway up the side of the windward face.

"Anything?"

He grumbles for a moment and manages an audible, "Nope."

"Me neither. Wanna swap?"

He steps out and nods as I complete my inspection of the circumference. Quince heads off in the direction I arrived from, and I step inside. Wow, what a difference. Just getting out of the wind warms me up several degrees.

Starting on my right, I perform a diligent visual scan. Nothing has been damaged. Fishing pole hangs from its hook, and the only item that seems disturbed is the chair, which previously held the body. I don't plan on touching that.

A voice penetrates the thin boards. "Find anything?"

As I'm about to call out "no joy," a strange pull tugs at my extra senses. Twisting the handle of the tiny wood-burning stove, I open the door and a heavy scent of smoke hits me. I'm not sure why this has my senses all atingle, but something isn't right.

"Hey, come here a second."

Quince's bright-red nose and wind-whipped watery eyes appear in the doorway. "What is it?"

"Not sure. I know this is going to sound weird, but something feels funny about the stove. It smells really smoky."

My young sidekick chuckles. "You know it burns wood, right?"

Standing and placing a hand on my hip, I shake my head. "Not helpful. Tell me how it works."

He rolls his eyes and looks at me as though I'm crazy. "You put the wood in, you throw in some birch bark or newspaper, light a match, and feed the fire. A lot of guys use pellets. My uncle was a purist."

The shock of the lengthy response catches me off guard.

He leans in the doorway. "Does that make sense?"

Nodding, I step closer to the stove. "This handle, on the straight piece of pipe, is that the flue?"

He nods. "Yeah. And you always crack a window to keep the airflow going. It's a small space—"

Our eyes meet, and our combined gaze shoots toward the secured window.

Quince is the first to voice our concern. "He wouldn't run the stove with the window closed."

"Is there a chance he was fishing without a fire going?"

He shakes his head vigorously. "You heard how cold it got that night. The sun woulda barely been peeking over the horizon when he got here after the first milking. There's no way he didn't start a fire."

"The rag!"

Quince tilts his head like a confused puppy. "The what?"

Pushing past him, I exit the icehouse and stumble toward the left side where the stovepipe exits the structure.

"Mitzy, what are you doing?" The photojournalist stares at me with concern. Rising to my tip-toes, I shove my arm, mitten and all, into the pipe. A second later, I yank it out and dangle the filthy rag. "Ta dah! Someone wanted to make sure smoke couldn't get out. I wonder if your uncle died of smoke inhalation, and the freezing came after?"

His entire demeanor changes. Quince steps back and rubs a gloved hand over his mouth as he shakes his head. "Carbon monoxide."

"What's that now?"

He continues to shake his head as he replies. "The closed window, the blocked stovepipe. Even a small fire would burn up the oxygen in there in no time." He sniffles, looks away, and his voice is barely a whisper. "At least I've heard carbon monoxide poisoning is painless."

Without thinking, I walk toward the boy and wrap my arms around him.

Him not pulling away is testament to the im-pact of our discovery.

"Should we take the evidence to Erick?"

Quince nods. "If we leave it here, someone could come back and take it. I'll get my camera and snap a few pics. The closed window is as important as that rag."

He retrieves his camera, which likely cost more than his entire hooptie. Which is what we call a beat-up, janky, piece-of-trash vehicle.

While he documents the scene, I attempt to gather additional information from the filthy fabric.

No such luck.

"I'm done. Let's hit it."

"Hold on, I have to put the crime-scene tape back." Using the cheat of a psychic replay, I re-wrap the icehouse exactly as we found it. "There. Now no one will be the wiser."

"Cool. Maybe the sheriff can pull fingerprints off that rag."

Far be it from me to burst Quince's balloon, but I don't think they can pull prints from cloth. Although, there may be some particulates that will lead them to the killer.

One thing is for sure. There's no denying it now. Quade Knudsen was absolutely murdered.

CHAPTER 12

THE DEPUTY whom I've nicknamed Furious Monkeys occupies the front desk with her usual flair.

"Good morning, Deputy Baird."

Her eyes remain locked on the screen of her phone as she battles her way through another level of her favorite game. "He's in his office."

"Thanks."

As I push through the crooked wooden gate separating the front waiting area from the bullpen, a surprising voice pulls my attention back.

"Hey, what level are you?" Quince rests his elbows on the counter and glances at the deputy's screen.

She grins. "Just crushed 328."

"Cool. I'm 330."

The shock that grips Baird's face is palpable. "You're Superbomb? The only one to crack 330?"

Quince makes a poor attempt at hiding his smirk. "Yeah. Mad respect though, GunandBadge."

She accepts the compliment, nods, and watches her virtual-opponent-come-to-life follow me toward Erick's office.

Deputy Gilbert taps away on a typewriter and barely looks up as we pass. It still shocks me to see someone typing at an actual typewriter! But it shouldn't. After all, this is the town that tech forgot. And things like old-fashioned paper passbooks at the bank and a majority of businesses that take cash only are par for the course around here.

Whispering over my shoulder, I can't resist gathering more gaming intel from Quince. "How long have you been playing that game?"

"Since the beginning, dude. I'm an OG."

I stop in my tracks and turn toward the photo-journalist, who continues to surprise me. "OG? You, my young friend, are about as far from an original gangster as one could get."

He scrunches up his face and shakes his head. "No, dude. It's true. No numbers after my handle. All the solid names are taken now. So the noobs have to steal good handles and add numbers to make a unique username."

I feign a curtsy. "Well, I beg your pardon, good Sir Superbomb."

He scoffs and flicks his wrist at me. "Let's get this over with."

We continue into Erick's office, and the second I walk through the door without my crutch, he's on his feet, shaking a finger in my direction. "Moon! You're not supposed to put any weight on it."

Lifting my hands in the air as though it's a stickup, I jump to my own defense. "Easy, officer. I'm unarmed. And I'm un-crutched."

He pounds his fist on a stack of papers on his desk and shakes his head. "What emergency caused you to take this risk with your own health?"

"It's not that big of a risk, Erick. This walking boot thingy is doing all the work. I'm keeping most of the weight off it." I quickly shift to my right leg to make good on my claim.

Before he can offer any further admonishment, Quince jumps in. "We found some evidence."

Erick chuckles coldly and presses a hand to his forehead. "Do I even want to know?"

"Don't worry, we didn't disturb anything inside. This rag was shoved in the open end of the stovepipe at Quade's icehouse."

I can almost hear the wheels turning behind Erick's intense blue eyes as he adds this clue to his list. "Hm, there would be no reason for them to check for carbon monoxide. Normally, the bright pinkish-red color of a corpse gives immediate visual indication. However, the freezing of the body would've canceled that out. Whoever set this up knew how to cover their tracks." He grabs an evidence bag from a box on the dented file cabinet behind his desk. "Drop that in here."

As I place the filthy piece of cloth in the evidence bag, I can't resist a little sass. "Sir, yes, sir."

"Sorry, Moon. I appreciate you bringing the evidence in, but I wish you'd stay away from my crime scenes."

I offer him a pouty frown. "But I help you."

"It's not that. I'd just love for you to take care of that foot like it matters."

Shrugging, I avoid his gaze. "I'm a fast healer."

He chuckles and rubs a hand across his mouth. I'm not sure what he's hoping to prevent himself from saying, but I suppose I'll take it as a gift. "You two run across anything else?"

"This and a tightly closed window, but that's all so far, Sheriff." I place a hand on my hip and flash him a smile with a bonus wink.

"Okay, then. Thanks again. I'll get in touch with the medical examiner, and if we can confirm elevated levels of carbon monoxide that could give us a new lead."

"What about the rag? Can you run it for particulates?"

He crosses his arms in that way that always distracts me from the matter at hand. "Don't worry, Moon. I still know how to run an investigation, despite the fact that I have amateurs clamoring to take over my department at every turn."

At least he laughs after he says it, and I add my forced chuckle to the mix.

"You'll let us know what the ME finds out, right?"

He drops the evidence bag on his desk, places both hands on the surface, and exhales with force. "I feel like that's a foregone conclusion."

"Good. Let me know if you want to meet up for coffee later."

Turning, I poke Quince a couple of times and nod my head toward the exit. I get it. He's young. He hasn't learned the art of how to quit while you're ahead. I happen to know that even a noncommittal promise of a peek at the medical examiner's report is the best I'm going to get on this visit. My plan is to hightail it out of the station before I say anything to kill my advantage.

Quince shuffles forward but grumbles over his shoulder. "Okay, okay, you don't have to go aggro."

I hardly think my gentle nudging is aggressive behavior, but I'll let the matter drop. Unfortunately, the mere discussion of coffee has got my stomach grumbling. "Want to grab some grub at the diner?"

"Nah. Gotta get back and help my dad."

"Copy that. I'll let you know what I hear from Erick."

"Sweet."

He dives into his rust-bucket truck, and I head toward french-fry heaven.

Seems like an off time of day to visit the diner and traffic is light. Instead of a booth, I choose a stool at the counter, so it will be easier to chat with my grandfather. Plus, my foot is throbbing like a . . . So I elevate it on the next stool. I should've taken some pain meds to go.

Odell grins through the orders-up window and offers me a spatula salute. The oil in the fryer sizzles as the basket of fries drops in.

The whole frozen cheesemaker thing has kinda put me off dairy. I open my mouth to mention I'd like to skip the cheese on my burger. But then a sneaky little part of me wants to test my theory about his possible psychic abilities, so I press my lips together and keep my cheesy secret to myself.

Tally's daughter Tatum is covering the afternoon shift today. She lazily wipes the counter in front of me and smiles. "Mom said you were helping Quince Knudsen. Are you two friends?"

"If you could call it that." On the surface, her

question seems innocent enough, but my extrasensory perception picks up on something beneath. "He's helped me on a case or two in the past. Quince has the inside track on what goes on around here—with all of his years working at the paper."

Relief loosens her shoulders, and she ceases the pretense of cleaning the counters. "Oh, cool. He's like super good at taking pictures, right?"

Well, now anyone with half a brain can see she's more than a fan of his photos. "Mmhmm. He was in here the other day, but I don't think your mom was working . . ." I leave the unspoken question hanging in the air and I'm rewarded with the gentle blush of her cheeks as she looks down and rearranges the salt, pepper, and ketchup.

"Oh, yeah. He comes in sometimes. You know, the paper is just up the street."

Odell interrupts our visit as he slides my plate of food onto the counter.

My mouth opens slowly and I point to my cheese-*less* burger. "How did you know?"

He grins mischievously, winks, and raps his knuckles twice on the counter before returning to the grill without a word.

That settles it. I don't need to run any more tests. That man may not know he has some kind of supernatural ability, but there's no way he can occupy a branch in my family tree without at least a trickle of something in his veins.

"I'm about to demolish this burger, Tatum. Why don't you tell me how long you've had a crush on Quince, and if there's anything I can do to move things forward, while I power through this deliciousness?"

Her eyes widen and she starts to shake her head, but as the hint of pink in her cheeks shifts to a darker red, she nods and giggles. "I should've known better than to talk about him in front of you. My mom says you're 'special.'"

My mouth is way too full of golden french fries to argue with her use of the word special. I attempt to pass off a confused shrug and gesture for her to continue.

She glances over her shoulder at Odell, who kindly pretends to be too busy to notice her not working, and fills me in on the particulars. "Like, I was a senior when he was a sophomore, so even though I thought he was super talented and, you know, hot, it wasn't cool to let anyone know. You know how high school is, right?"

I roll my eyes and nod.

Tatum shrugs. "So, you get it. Then I went away to college, and I was only home on breaks. It's not like I could go trolling around the high school. That would be super lame."

Swallowing quickly, I gulp down some soda and squeeze in a reply. "Yeah, I get it. I think you made the right call."

She nods confidently. "But once he graduated, I'd see him in the diner. I was on break . . . He was on break. You know?"

Boy, did I know. When I think back to how my relationship with Erick started with me being a suspect and turned into me being a practically respectable consultant . . . I completely understand. Take whatever opportunity the Fates hand you. "Does he talk to you? Because he can barely be bothered to put two words together when I ask him questions."

That information brightens her smile nearly a thousand watts. "Um, he totally talks to me. He was telling me all about his dark-room setup, and his camera, and, like, this thesis project he's working on for some self-directed program at Columbia."

My eyes twinkle and I smile as I lean forward. "Are you into cameras or dark rooms?"

Tatum giggles and shakes her head. "Not really, but I just like to hear him talk."

I smile and nod at her strategy. "That's not a bad plan. I went to a broomball game, tried cross-country skiing, and even attended the Renaissance Faire in an attempt to make some headway with the men in my life." We share a laugh. "What would you say is your best move?"

She takes one more nervous glance over her shoulder and leans extra close. "Sometimes I give him free milkshakes."

My whole face lights up as I imagine the joy that must bring my penny-pinching photo source. "That's a super good idea. Does he know you like him?"

She stands up and tucks a loose strand of hair behind her ear. "Well—you know—um—I'm sure he probably thinks I'm friendly. But, like, I *like* him, like him."

That's a lot to unpack. "I'll see what I can do."

She blanches, and the color drains from her face as her eyes widen. "Don't tell him I told you."

I tilt my head and smirk. "Hey, I'm special, remember. I got you."

She gasps and I can sense her heart racing. "Okay, but, like, be cool."

If you assume that my mind instantly goes to the John Travolta movie, you're right. *Get Shorty* may have been the vehicle that facilitated his comeback, but *Be Cool* solidified it.

"Did you hear what I said, Mitzy? You can, like, be cool about it, right?"

"Ice cold. No worries."

She giggles nervously and reaches out to bus my dishes.

"See ya 'round, Gramps."

Odell shakes his head and chuckles. "If you two hens are done clucking, I need a word, Mitzy."

Uh oh. I hope I'm not in trouble. I can't think of anything I've done to draw his wrath, but acting without thinking is one of my hidden talents.

When I step into the kitchen, Odell sets down his burger flipper and steps toward me. "Hey, you're looking into the murder of that Knudsen kid's uncle. I thought you should know, him and his neighbor have had a long-standing property feud. Quade seemed to be particular about everything in his life except fence repair. And that neighbor got awful tired of the cows ransacking his cornfield. I heard him complaining to beat the devil over his coffee more than once. I'm not saying the guy's mad enough to murder somebody, but it never hurts to have another suspect, right?"

I cross my arms and grin with satisfaction. "So, Grams was right."

"About what?"

"Snooping runs in the family."

CHAPTER 13

I USUALLY BLAME my bad decisions on an empty stomach, or alcohol. But, I have to admit, I'm making this one sober and fully fed. Plus I slipped into the apartment and got some pain meds, so I feel invincible-adjacent.

My ankle pain has downgraded from throbbing to a dull ache. Most people would take that as a good sign, and continue to follow their doctor's orders. I, however, take it as a sign from the powers that be that I need to pursue this investigation with renewed vigor. This fresh lead about the neighbor must be handled.

Erick has his hands full with the recent evidence Quince and I provided, and the medical examiner is still waiting for confirmation of the time of death from that lab down south. Looks like it's time for me to hop in my vehicle and pay Quade's neighbor a visit.

At least I toss my crutch in the backseat, in case of emergency.

A quick text to Odell results in a surprisingly rapid response. Apparently, he likes to cluck as much as the hens. He sends me the neighbor's name and directions to the property, without a single warning or "take it easy."

I'm certainly not one to play favorites, but right now Gramps is at the top of my Most Awesome People list.

Sadly, the weather has no interest in "best of" lists and takes one of its notorious sudden turns for the worse. The sky that moments ago sported puffy white clouds is now thick with ominous grey warning.

Things definitely don't improve when I turn down the narrow county road which dead-ends at Herman Pettit's corn farm. It's a struggle to keep out of the snowbanks pressing in on either side of the single-track lane. On the plus side, the defrost on the new Jeep actually works, and I can see out the front window.

I'm not sure how much traffic uses this road, but I turn on my headlights just in case.

There can't possibly be any harvesting to handle or seeds to plant in the middle of winter, so

I'm hoping I'll find Herman tucked in his cozy abode.

After letting myself in through the screen door that accesses the three-season porch, I knock politely on the front door of the modest two-story farmhouse.

No answer.

A second, louder knock produces no response.

Thanks, universe. Why make it easy for the girl who's hopping along on one and three-quarter legs.

Glancing around the extensive property, I take note of several outbuildings, including a well-maintained barn.

Before I attempt the lengthy trek to where I hope to find the man I'm looking for, I grab my *emergency* crutch from the Jeep.

As I hobble along, the scent of burning wood hits me. About the same time I see the puffs rising from a small round pipe on the barn's roof.

In the movies, people always slide or pull open the giant doors at the end of the barn for a dramatic reveal. There's no way I'm going to try a stunt like that with a crutch and a somewhat bum foot. I opt for the smaller, human-sized door to the left.

It's unlocked. Will wonders never cease?

There's someone in the barn, busily wrenching away under something that could be a combine harvester, or a *Tyrannosaurus rex*, for all I know about farming equipment.

Rather than surprise him and take a chance on an unfriendly welcome, I call out politely. "Mr. Pettit? Mr. Pettit, it's Mitzy Moon from the Bell, Book & Candle. I hate to interrupt you—"

He rolls out from under the massive piece of equipment on one of those low-to-the-ground mechanic's creepers. I know the official name of the item because of a failed student film that attempted to re-create a dangerous scene from a *Charlie's Angels* movie. I mean, everyone lived, but barely.

Herman is a red-haired man with a carefully waxed mustache that smells of tobacco and leather, and he's far younger than I expected. Mid-thirties, stout, with strong hands and keen eyes. "Broken or sprained?" he asks.

If I had a nickel for every time I'd answered that question in the last few days, I'd be a— Oh wait, seems like I'm already as wealthy as anyone would need to be. Pasting on my best fake grin, I offer up a congenial response. "It's a bad sprain. Folks tell me I'd have been better off with a break. But I'm not sure I agree."

He wipes his hands on a red rag tucked in the pocket of his work pants and nods. "A sprain might hurt a little more in the beginning, but it will heal faster in the end. Don't listen to those fools. People are always so eager to repeat every nonsense old wives' tale they've ever been told. What can I do you for?"

I wish I could say that's the first time I've heard that folksy twist of the phrase since I came to Pin Cherry, but it's absolutely not. However, far be it from me to say anything to Herman Pettit that might indicate he's following the crowd. He obviously takes his hipster farming duties quite seriously. "Well, like I said, I'm Mitzy Moon. I help the local sheriff on a case-by-case basis. So you're under no obligation to cooperate with me or answer any questions, but I heard you're the man to talk to about what goes on in these parts, and I need a shortcut to some answers."

The respectful tone combined with some subtle flattery seems to do the trick. Herman glances around, takes the compliment in stride, and nods for me to continue.

"I understand you've had some trouble with cattle getting into your property and damaging crops. Is it all from the same herd, or are there multiple offenders?"

At first, his gaze is suspicious, but his burning need to be heard wins out. "Well, I tell you what, I filed more than one complaint with the sheriff, or whatever deputy he sends out to humor me. Nothing ever happens, though. The cows keep breaking through different parts of that fence and my crops keep payin' the price. I guess that's what passes for justice in this backwater town."

"I'm sorry to hear that, Mr. Pettit. Do you recall who repaired the fence, or fences?"

That does the trick.

"Oh, it was always the same flippin' fence! Pardon my French. I was the one who had to handle the repairs. Now, I'm not saying I'm an expert. I've only been working this land for five years, but what could I do? Prim and proper Quade sure wasn't gonna fix it. I did the best I could, but his cattle are strong and stubborn. Once they make it through, they just keep coming. Cost me thousands! Thousands of dollars that I don't have! Not one of those complaints I filed ever amounted to a hill of beans."

"That's a real shame. If you like, I'd be happy to look into those complaints and see if there's anything I can do."

The bait has officially been dangled. There's a strange shift in his energy, and my psychic senses can't decide if it's regret or relief.

"Well, I'm not sure what anyone can do about it now. I heard Quade Knudsen froze to death in his icehouse. I suppose that so-called partner of his will finally get to sell the whole operation."

My mood ring tingles and I glance down in time

to see a wheel of cheese. Not that the image does me much good, but there was something about the way Herman said "so-called partner" that could do with a follow-up. "Gosh, it's good to hear your tribulations will be over, Mr. Pettit. Thank you for your time today. I'll see myself out."

As I twist around my crutch and head for the small door, he calls out. "Hold on, Miss Moon."

I pause, and he rummages through a tall metal cabinet at the end of his workbench.

"It's only a sample size, but I sure appreciate you looking into things." He hands over a small plastic bag closed with a red twist tie at the top.

When I catch sight of the label, I have to chuckle. "Pop's Corn!" A huge red handlebar mustache cradles the name. "I love it. Thank you, Mr. Pettit, or should I say Pop? Looks like a storm's comin'. You take care."

As I trudge through the snow, back toward my vehicle, the only thing that stands out about that conversation is how I'm sounding more and more like a local each day. Look at me, talking about the weather and getting popcorn samples!

Time to get back to the bookshop before anyone figures out what I've been up to.

Whoever said "the best laid plans of mice and men" has absolutely met my grandmother. Before the alleyway door can even close behind me, she's already schooling me about taking additional risks driving with my concussed head.

"I understand your concern, Grams. But would it make things better if I told you I have another suspect to add to the murder board?"

She taps a finger on one of her strands of pearls and chews the inside of her cheek. "It might. What did you discover?"

"Your new boyfriend gave me a tip." The giggles grip me almost immediately. I'd hoped to hold a poker face for at least a few seconds, but no such luck.

"Are you talking about Odell? He's not my boyfriend, Mitzy. He's my ex-husband, and he's human!"

"So are you—sort of."

She pushes my suggestion away with a wave of her hand. "Psh. Tosh. I'm an earthbound spirit. A ghost. Not in the least human!"

"Sometimes, when you're not having a tantrum, you can take corporeal form. I'd say you're sort of more human-*light* than ghost."

This new concept clearly intrigues her. She floats up toward the Rare Books Loft and passes through the thick balustrade.

I negotiate the dangerous spiral staircase and chain, and meet her in the apartment.

"Human-light? That has a nice ring to it, dear.

However, my days of husbands and special friends are over. I'm grateful for Odell's company, but part of me is sad that he lacks genuine human companionship in his own life."

"His diner is full of people, Grams. Maybe he never remarried, but it's his own choice. I think he actually prefers solitude."

"Well, you're the psychic, sweetie." And with that, she grabs a pen off the coffee table and hovers above our stack of 3 x 5 cards.

"Make a card for Herman Pettit. He's a young popcorn farmer that shares a property line with the deceased."

"Oh, well, property disputes can be deadly. Has he taken possession of the disputed land now that Quade's out of the picture?"

"Um, it wasn't exactly that kind of property dispute. Quade's cows are always breaking through the fence and getting into the popcorn farmer's field."

Grams suffers an attack of the ghost giggles and distracts me from my careful explanation. "I'm sorry, dear. You have to stop saying popcorn farmer. All I can picture is some Wild West cartoon cowboy with a giant handlebar mustache riding through his fields attempting to lasso giant pieces of popped corn as they shoot into the air like Roman candles."

"You're half right, about the mustache at least, but what's a Roman candle?"

"Sweetie, I forget how young you are. Back in the days before unending frivolous lawsuits, a lot of things were unregulated. Roman candles were a powerful type of firework. Practically as impressive as the huge displays the municipalities used to put on. We would take one of those things, shove it in the ground, light the fuse, and colorful rockets would fire hundreds of feet into the air. It was fantastic."

"Sounds fabulous, but it's not something that would get a lot of support in a state that's primarily desert—and suffers from its own set of massive wildfires almost every year. But I can picture it." Closing my eyes, I picture my grandmother's words, and, for a moment, I see a night sky exploding with color.

"It's magnificent, Grams."

She hums softly and sighs with memory. "Please continue your story, dear."

"All right, and I agree to stop using the term popcorn farmer. I'll stick with the farmer, or possibly the corn farmer. Even though he has the most adorable name for his product." Reaching into the pocket of my puffy jacket, which is draped over the back of the settee, I extract the sample and turn the label toward Grams.

She squeals and covers her mouth with one hand. "Oh, that's clever. You should invest in his company straightaway. I'm telling you, that Mr. Pettit is going places."

"He might be, but I think I'll wait until we take him off the suspect list before I give him any money. Sound good?"

She taps her shimmering finger to the side of her head and smiles. "You're exactly as smart as you look."

"Thanks, Grams. Herman seems like an exceptionally calm man, and he answered my questions without any hassle, but something felt off. He said he's filed several complaints with the sheriff's department about the cow intrusions, but Erick never mentioned anything about a dispute with a neighbor."

"Maybe the man was lying. You know, sweetie, people will say anything when they're under suspicion."

"But I didn't accuse him of anything. I didn't even bring up Mr. Knudsen's death. He's the one who brought up the incident, and my psychic antenna didn't pick up on dishonesty."

"Maybe the pain meds are blocking your messages."

"Wait? How did you—?"

"You left them out on the counter in the bathroom. I noticed a few more were missing. You can hardly call it snooping when it's right out in the open."

"Accurate."

She shrugs and offers a semi-apologetic smile.

"I'll stop taking them and see if I can manage. I don't think there's been any side effects, but we should play it safe, right?"

"I agree, dear. We know what happens when you're cut off from your powers." She shudders with an unpleasant memory.

"I need to call Erick and let him know what I uncovered. Maybe he's had time to talk to Tammy."

"Who's Tammy? We don't have a card for her."

"We better make one. She's part of Oscar's alibi."

Grams, dutiful as ever, makes a card for Tammy and floats it toward me. Tacking it on the board, I run a connecting piece of green yarn from her to Oscar and a second one from her to Quade. If the weekly suppers were a reality and not a fabrication, she was definitely acquainted with the deceased.

Grams nods thoughtfully. "I absolutely agree."

Turning, I point a finger to my lips and shake my head. "Even though you shouldn't be agreeing, because I didn't say anything out loud."

"You were facing away, Mitzy! There was absolutely no way for me to make visual confirmation. I heard what you said, and I assumed the lips were moving."

With a heavy exhale, I hobble back to the settee. "I'll allow it."

"Thank you for your leniency, dear." She snickers and swirls toward me.

"Oh brother."

Retrieving my cell phone from my coat, I place a call to Erick on speakerphone. There's no point trying to have a private conversation with a ghost circling around me like a possessed carnival ride.

"Hey, Mitzy, do you need something?"

Mmm mm, that voice. My initial instinct is to tell him exactly what I need. The eavesdropping ghost of my dear grandmother prevents me.

She winks at me and grins wickedly.

"Nothing I can announce in front of present company. You're on speakerphone."

He chuckles. "10-4."

"I called to give you an update. Apparently, Quade had some serious disputes with the farmer who owns the adjacent property."

"Herman Pettit? Do you mean to tell me you drove out to his farm in your condition?"

"Why does everyone keep saying that? I sprained my ankle, I didn't fracture my spine!"

"Let's not tempt fate, Moon. What did you find out?"

"Herman claims he's filed a series of complaints with your office. He acted like he'd spoken to you directly about the problem of Quade's cows and had several subsequent discussions with your deputies. But you didn't mention he could be a suspect. Why?"

Erick pauses, draws a sharp breath in through his teeth, and continues. "I believe I spoke to him the first time. And I can't honestly say how many other reports he may have filed. Complaints like his are considered nuisance complaints. They're usually followed up by the deputy with the least seniority on the force at the time. They're seldom, if ever, given any sort of—"

"Oh, I get it. Some kook growing popcorn has an issue with cows, and the local sheriff doesn't take it seriously."

Grams hovers in front of me and wags a finger. "More flies with honey."

I wave her away and frown.

Erick exhales loudly. "It's not like that, Moon. Things have to be prioritized. His issues may not have gotten the attention they deserved, because of other more serious issues. I'll have Deputy Johnson pull the file and see if we missed something. I appreciate the tip."

"Anytime, Sheriff." I offer a break in the conversation for him to reciprocate, but nothing is forth-coming. Not a problem. I'm happy to pry.

Ghostly chuckles from across the room offer no argument.

"Did you question Tammy?"

"Not yet. I'm not sure if it's worth our time."

"What? It's absolutely worth your time. Oscar's entire statement basically hinges on Tammy con-firming his alibi."

"Not to pull the *sheriff* card, but this is my in-vestigation, and I'm not sure what you mean, Moon. We don't have time of death yet, so we're not con-firming alibis."

"All right. You got me on a technicality, Sheriff. But he said the plans to subcontract for some big dairy down south were made by him and Quade. Seems like you should confirm that with Tammy before he has a chance— Never mind. I'm sure the first thing he did when he got home was to tell her exactly what he said. That watering hole's already been poisoned."

"If he told us the truth, she already knew about the planned sale." Erick's tone takes on a defensive edge, but I do like that he said "us."

"You might have a point."

"That's better, sweetie. Kill him with kindness." Grams grins.

A moment of pensive silence hangs in the air.

"I'm gonna see if Quince will take me out to the dairy." Inhaling deeply, I prepare to end the call.

"Look, Moon, that might not be a crime scene, but I don't need you poking around—"

"What? You're breaking up. I'll try to call you later."

End.

"Mitzy, I'm surprised at you. Why would you take such a tone with Erick? He only has your best interests at heart." Grams crosses her arms over her ample bosom and arches one brow.

"I don't know. My ankle hurts and I need a solid lead." Struggling to my feet, I hobble toward the bathroom and my pain meds. Despite the warning from Grams, I take two to get ahead of the pain curve.

A quick text to Quince secures me a guided tour of the dairy.

CHAPTER 14

UDDERLY BRILLIANT IS NOT what I expected! I pictured a couple of cows with big bells around their necks, a hand-hewn three-legged stool, and a stainless-steel milk pail. What I discovered is that this dairy is next level.

Quade may have insisted on keeping an artisan feel, but his morning milking did not involve hands-on contact with Bessie, or any of the other five hundred cows housed at *Udderly Brilliant*.

The barn, if you can call it that, is an industrial-grey building constructed entirely of metal beams and corrugated metal siding. Inside, five concrete platforms stretch the length of the barn and are divided into individual stalls with dedicated milking equipment for each. All the "milkers" feed into a massive collection tank. To be honest, it's a little *Matrix*-y.

"This place is huge."

Quince nods his head and follows that gesture with a lackluster shrug. "Not compared to the big-time players down south."

I'll take his word for it. After passing through the large harvesting area, he leads me into a much smaller back room with shelving units that reach above my head, and large stainless steel sinks.

"What's this area for?"

"Uncle Quade never used any growth hormones, but his cows were on a vitamin regimen and some got special additives to their food specifically for the flavors that would be passed on to the cheese."

Wow! His verbosity is throwing me for a loop. Either he's really into making cheese, or he's taking this investigation more seriously than I thought possible. "But how do you keep it straight, with that octopus milking monstrosity?"

He grins knowingly. "The Classy Gals, as my uncle nicknamed them, were milked separately."

Ah ha, now I'm going to see my three-legged stool and movie-trope milk pail. "Before you show me that room, is this some kind of cleanup station?"

"Pretty much. Any sterilizing of equipment or individual feed troughs would be done here." He points to a sturdy shelf above the sink and opens his mouth to speak. No words come out. Consternation squeezes his eyes to slits, and he shakes his head in disagreement with whatever's going on in his mind.

"What is it?"

"Quade would never leave the chlorine bleach and the phosphoric acid open at the same time. He was very careful with his chemicals. Mixing those two together could create chlorine gas."

"That sounds deadly."

"In the right quantity, yah." Quince nods and moves to put the caps back on the containers.

"Don't touch anything. I'm calling Erick right now. I know it doesn't seem like much, but it's not how your uncle would've left things, and we have precious little to go on right now. It could be a clue."

Quince nods and passes his carefully trained photographer's eye over every inch of the space. He snaps a couple pictures on his phone while I inform Erick of our find.

The sheriff is asking a series of questions, which I have no intention of answering, so I cover the phone with one hand and whisper sharply to Quince. "What are you doing? You don't take digital pics."

He glances at me and frowns. "These aren't for the paper."

"Copy that."

"What? No, I was talking to Quince, not you. I was distracted. You really should come and take a look at this. We'll keep poking around. See ya soon."

I end the call before he can instruct me to get back into my vehicle. Approaching the sink area, I take a focusing breath and reach out with my psychic gifts.

Nada. Bupkus.

"Mitzy, what are you doing?"

"Oh, um. Just looking around. You know, to see if anything catches my eye."

He shrugs. "I'll show you the Classy Gals' suite."

We step into the adjacent mini-sized milking room, which contains two stalls and what appears to be its own collection tank. The room is sterile, but cozy.

"Was this your uncle's personal project? Would anyone else have milked the cows?"

Quince scrunches up his face and shakes his head. "Very particular, remember?"

"Got it. So anyone who knew your uncle's routine would know that this would be the last stop on his daily schedule."

"Yah."

I may be an amateur sleuth, but I'm not even close to an amateur cheesemaker. Nothing seems out of order, and my moody mood ring is no help.

My tour guide steps closer than he's ever dared and points to the collection tank. "That should be empty."

"Why?"

"The milk should be in the Processing Room. Uncle Quade would never leave it in a collection tank."

"Seems like we have two things for the sheriff to look at when he gets here." I nod my head with more confidence than I feel.

Quince glances around the room and bites his lower lip. "The deputies were already here. But if they weren't familiar with the process, they wouldn't have noticed stuff like the chemicals, or this milk."

While we wait for Erick or one of his deputies to show up, Oscar Wiggins tromps into the room with the sinks, and, when he sees us returning from the Classy Gals' suite, his jaw falls slack.

Quince offers a halfhearted wave. "Hey, Mr. Wiggins."

"Oh, hello. You're the nephew, right?"

Quince nods, and I hop forward to introduce myself. "I'm Mitzy Moon. We haven't met." Technically, I know who he is, because I eavesdropped on his interview at the sheriff's station, but he doesn't know that. There's a hint of tobacco about his person, and I lean in with my outstretched hand to get a better whiff. Something familiar, but I can't place it.

He smiles but doesn't offer to shake my hand. "You'll have to excuse me, I need to wash my hands." He steps toward the sink and the open chemical containers, and Quince and I exchange a worried glance.

Once Oscar finishes with the soap and water, he grabs a paper towel and turns toward us with a shrug. "Was there something I can help you with? I don't think your uncle kept any of his personal effects out here."

It almost sounds defensive, but no hairs are tingling on the back of my neck, and I'm not getting any hits to my super senses. "Oh, we're waiting for Sheriff Harper."

He crinkles the paper towel in his hands with unnecessary force and the muscles in his jaw flex. "He's headed out here?"

My eyes dart toward Quince and he shakes his head almost imperceptibly.

Time to play dumb and see how far that gets me. "Yeah, actually I'm a consultant with the department and I'm looking into a local theft." I have no idea where I'm going with this.

Oscar lifts his chin and carefully strokes his goatee. "Theft? What brings you to the dairy?"

He has asked an excellent question and I have

absolutely no answer. Think. Think. Think. My mind is a total blank. What the heck is wrong with me?

Quince steps forward. "She's not looking into the theft here. She just bummed a ride off me." He gestures to my leg. "I needed some pictures for the paper before I drop her off." Lifting his cell phone, he wiggles it back and forth.

Oscar nods. "Oh, that's okay. Just keep it tasteful. We don't want any negative publicity to ruin the sale."

My mouth opens before my brain has time to engage. "Sale? I thought it was a sub-producing contract?"

The dairy owner's gaze narrows, and he steps toward me. "Where did you hear that?"

Great, another excellent question I can't answer.

Quince saves me once again. "She works with the sheriff. You know how it is in a small town."

The explanation seems to appease Oscar. He still looks a shade suspicious, but I'm not getting any kind of weird vibe. "Well, you two had better see yourselves out. I've got to attend to that gosh darn fence before hot-headed Herman Pettit starts waving his shotgun around again."

My mouth starts to open, but a firm hand grips my arm. Quince is actually willing to touch me, of his own free will. It must be important. I take the hint and keep my mouth shut.

Oscar strides back into the vast milking operation and disappears out the far door.

Quince lowers his voice. "He didn't even notice the chemicals were open."

"Yeah, and he thinks you take pictures with your phone. He's clearly not real observant. Plus, if he'd been up to no good, his conscience would've caused him to at least glance toward the shelf."

Quince pulls away and scrapes a hand through his long bangs. "You okay on your own for a minute?"

I shrug. "Probably. Where are you going?"

"Need to check on something. I'll be back in, like, two minutes." He grabs a stool from the small milking room and helps me lower myself onto it.

"Thanks."

He nods and jogs off in the opposite direction from Oscar.

Meanwhile, as luck would have it, Deputy Paulsen shows up and waddles into the barn.

I offer a friendly wave from my three-legged seat and she returns my gesture with a scowl and a firmer grip on the handle of her holstered gun.

As she approaches, the sound of polyester rubbing against itself grows louder. "What kind of trouble have you gotten yourself into now, Moon?"

"No trouble. I came out here with Quince, so he could pay his respects to his dearly departed uncle. Apparently, Quade was very particular about the way he did things. The same routine, always the same sequence of events. You get the idea."

She nods with irritation. "This little story got a point?"

Using the tip of my crutch, I gesture to the two open chemical containers on the shelf. "That's chlorine bleach and that one's phosphoric acid. Both used in cleaning and maintenance of various systems around the dairy, but they should never be mixed together, because—"

"Yeah, chlorine gas. We all took high school chemistry."

"All right. My point is, you found an empty bourbon bottle at the crime scene, but Quade didn't drink. Alcohol would've reacted with his medication. Everyone assumed he passed out and froze to death. What if someone used some other method to knock him out and planted him in the icehouse with that decoy bottle to make it look like an accident?"

She runs her tongue over her top teeth and makes an impatient squeaking noise. "I thought your theory was carbon monoxide poisoning? Now you think somebody knocked him out with chlorine gas, got him liquored up, locked him in a fish house, sabotaged it so he would get carbon monoxide poisoning, and he froze to death on top of it? You really do have an active imagination, Moon."

This woman knows exactly how to push my buttons every single time she interacts with me. "Look, Paulsen, I'm trying to find a murderer. I think it's a little early in the investigation to be turning our back on any potential lead."

She opens her mouth to offer what I'm sure she thinks is a snappy retort, but a breathless Quince interrupts her delivery.

"She's dead!"

Without a moment's hesitation, Paulsen draws her weapon. "Show me."

Quince turns to lead the way, and I struggle to rise from the tiny stool. After two false starts, I finally get a low enough grip on the cross member of the crutch to create the right leverage point and pull my largesse from my tuffet.

Luckily, Deputy Paulsen and her short-legged stride are an easy target. With some expert crutching, I catch up in no time.

Quince leads us to the back of the barn and lifts a large black tarpaulin.

Paulsen groans and shakes her head.

I opt for a gasp and scream.

Oscar Wiggins comes barreling around the

corner of the barn and screeches to a halt when he sees Deputy Paulsen. "What's going on here?"

Paulsen holsters her gun, steps forward, and crosses her arms. "I'll be asking the questions, Wiggins. What happened to the heifer?"

"She didn't make it back to the barn, and when we had that terrible cold snap the other night—"

Quince is agitated, and he's not about to accept Wiggins' halfhearted explanation. "This is one of the Classy Gals, Wiggins. My uncle would never leave her out of the barn."

Wiggins' eyes dart to the bright pink X sprayed on the cow's right rear haunch, but he attempts to play dumb. "I don't know what you're talking about, kid. It's a cow. We have five hundred of them, you know. Sometimes they die. Cycle of life."

Quince turns to Deputy Paulsen. "I bet toxicology tests would show she died of chlorine gas poisoning."

Deputy Paulsen shakes her head and waves him off. "We don't do postmortems on bovines, kid."

I wait for my mood ring or one of my amazing psychic abilities to confirm Quince's idea, but nothing happens. Super. Well, my basic senses know a good idea when I hear one. If someone released chlorine gas in that small space in hopes of sedating or even killing Quade, the cow might've been a second, accidental victim. My fingers are already dialing the sheriff's station. Turning away, I give a brief but muffled explanation to Erick, and a moment later Deputy Paulsen's radio springs to life.

"Paulsen, Sheriff Harper here." She depresses the button on the side of the mic clipped to her shoulder. "Go for Paulsen."

"Tape off the area and get Johnson to pick up Doc Ledo's rig. Take the cow to his place and ask him to run toxicology."

Her shocked expression quickly turns to malice as she realizes I pulled rank. She scowls at me as she replies. "10-4."

Oscar puts up a fuss, but Paulsen threatens to throw him in handcuffs if he tries to interfere.

He wisely raises his hands, backs away, and disappears.

If I weren't on crutches, I would definitely give chase.

"You should wait inside, Mitzy. Do you need help?" Quince nods in my direction.

"No, I can manage. I'll go watch over the—"

Quince joins me in shouting, "The chemicals!"

CHAPTER 15

IN PURSUIT of the vanishing Oscar Wiggins, Quince easily outpaces me and my barely functioning tripod gait.

As I round the corner, raised voices echo through the vast barn.

"Don't touch that, Wiggins! I know you murdered my uncle!" A stool tips over and tools crash to the floor as a struggle ensues.

"Look, kid, I didn't kill anyone! Your uncle and I were partners. Get off me!"

I reach the back room just in time to witness Wiggins fling the wiry Quince across the room.

The young man's head crashes into a shelf.

He hits the ground and doesn't move.

Every ounce of film-school dropout inside of me begs for this one movie trope to be true. No matter how many times people get hit, or shot, or bang into things, they don't die. The hero always gets back up and keeps fighting.

Unfortunately, disappointment is the flavor du jour. Quince doesn't move. Oscar's eyes are wild, but before he can blurt his series of excuses, my fingers are already dialing.

Wiggins moves toward me with an angry growl. Lifting my crutch to create a physical barrier, I shake my head as I speak into the phone. "Sheriff Harper, Oscar Wiggins just attacked Quince Knudsen. Quince is unconscious in the barn at the *Udderly Brilliant* dairy. Please send an ambulance and more deputies."

Erick barely has time to announce that he's on his way before he ends the call, and less than twenty seconds later Paulsen enters the clean-up room with her weapon drawn. He must've radioed her as he ran to his patrol car.

"Hands where I can see 'em, Wiggins." She aims her gun dead center on the man's chest and tilts her head toward me. "Check the kid for a pulse, Moon."

My mouth hangs open and I'm left speechless. The idea that the impact killed Quince never entered my mind. Flinging my crutch to the side, I hobble-run toward his limp form. The two fingers on my left hand slide along his neck and thankfully find a pulse. "He's alive." My voice catches in my throat. I didn't realize how much I'd grown to care for this shutterbug.

Paulsen adjusts her aim and exhales loudly. "So it looks like just one murder charge for you, Wiggins."

He opens his mouth to protest, but she shakes her head and steadies the gun with threatening clarity. "Save it for the interrogation."

He swallows, shakes his head in disbelief, and keeps his hands in the air. She shifts her weapon to her right hand and retrieves the handcuffs from her duty belt. For a pudgy schoolyard bully, she moves with surprising speed. Oscar Wiggins is securely handcuffed and being led out of the building in under thirty seconds.

She glances over her shoulder. "I'm going to lock the accused in the back of the cruiser. Keep an eye on the kid. I hear the sirens. The ambulance will be here any minute." She shoves her quarry forward with more force than necessary, and I breathe a sigh of relief.

Although, I don't hear any sirens. Attempting to access my extrasensory hearing proves fruitless.

Instead, I focus on the unfortunate victim. "Hey, Quince. Can you hear me?" Brushing his sandy-brown bangs back from his face, I shake him gently.

No response.

I've seen enough crime drama to know that moving a victim is never a good idea for an amateur like me. I'll just wait helplessly until the paramedics arrive.

As if on cue, the wail of sirens pierces the winter air.

Erick makes it through the door before the emergency crew. "Moon, are you okay?"

"I'm fine. I mean, other than the sprained ankle and whatever from before. It's Quince. He's nonresponsive."

The sheriff drops to his knees next to the awkwardly sprawled young man and immediately checks for breathing and pulse. Before he can examine any further, the paramedics burst in and take over.

He offers me his hand, helps me to my feet, and retrieves my abandoned crutch.

Big, wet tears are welling up in my eyes. "I'll never forgive myself if—"

Erick slips an arm around my waist and kisses the top of my head. "Sounds like you're starting to understand how I feel every time you dive into one of these dangerous investigations."

I stifle a sob and gasp for air. "Don't lecture me, Sheriff."

He gives me a comforting squeeze. "It's not a

lecture, Moon. It's a reality check. Quince is young, and I'm sure he'll be fine. But if Oscar Wiggins is our murderer, things could've ended much worse."

The paramedics coordinate their lift of the stretcher and head for the ambulance.

Sheriff Harper salutes them and calls out, "I'll get in touch with his dad."

The young woman carrying the rear of the board nods in his direction and disappears into the main barn.

"Do you think he's gonna be all right? Wiggins tossed him pretty hard."

Erick scrunches up his face and shrugs. "I'm hoping he'll be fine. I need you to come in and make a statement, since you witnessed the assault."

"Sure, of course. Whatever you need. That man is clearly dangerous."

My boyfriend isn't as quick to agree as I'd hoped. Instead, he continues in sheriff-mode. "What brought on the physical altercation?"

"They were arguing. See those open chemicals on the shelf?"

Erick walks toward the shelf and takes in the potential meaning in a flash. "And?"

"Well, Quince and I were thinking that Oscar didn't know anything about the possible chlorine gas stuff, because when he came in to wash his hands, he didn't notice the open chemicals or even look at the shelves."

"Seems more likely that he purposely avoided looking at them to hide his possible guilt."

What Erick's saying does seem pretty logical. Why didn't my psychic senses give me a tipoff? The image of me throwing two pain pills down the hatch with half a glass of water comes to mind. What if Grams is right about the meds interfering with my gifts?

Erick is standing directly in front of me and leaning forward in concern. "Moon, are you having some concussion related issues?"

"No, just reviewing things in my mind. You know how I get."

He smiles. "That I do. Now what about this dead cow?"

I proceed to show him the Classy Gals' suite and crutch my way to the back of the barn so he can have a peek under the tarpaulin.

"We'll pick up the cow and see if Doc Ledo can determine cause of death. Meanwhile, we finally got confirmation on time of death from the big lab down south. Quade Knudsen died of carbon monoxide poisoning between 11:30 p.m. and 12:30 a.m. He subsequently froze before his body was discovered."

Leaning on my crutch, I lift my right finger, but

Erick waves away my question and continues. "They also found traces of chlorine in the lung tissue. Whoever tried to kill him was determined not to fail. They chose a hat trick of weapons."

My head spins with all this new information, and my empty stomach is swirling with the aftereffects of taking medication without food.

Since my ride headed into town in the back of an ambulance, Erick agrees to give me a lift back to the bookshop.

I wish I had the energy to convince him to grab some food for my upset stomach—which is quickly turning into nausea and a headache, but I'm fading fast. The best thing for me is a glass of water and some shuteye.

Grams is none too happy when I share the story of the mishap at the milk farm.

"Mizithra! You could've been killed." Tears spring to her eyes and she clutches her pearls as she sobs dramatically.

"Well, I wasn't. But Quince was definitely injured, and it was all my fault. I'm gonna take a quick nap and then I'll head over to the hospital to see how he's doing."

She opens her mouth to protest, but I wave my finger threateningly. "An innocent bystander almost died because of me. Me and my stupid twisted ankle. If I'd been able to drive myself out there, nothing would've happened to poor Quince. No more protests. I'm taking a nap, and then I'm going to the hospital, and I don't want to hear another word about it."

Ghost-ma pantomimes locking her lips with an invisible key and tucking it into her cleavage.

I don't have time for banter. After popping a couple pain pills, I drop my crutch on the thick Persian rug and collapse onto my bed.

Cut to —

Blackness. The kind of heavy darkness that envelops you in a damp, windless cave.

The throbbing in my ankle must have been the cause of my waking.

However, this nap started during the day, and it's clearly the middle of the moonless night. Not sure exactly what happened, but visiting hours are obviously over at the hospital. Probably best if I pop a few more pain pills and crash out until morning.

Using the post at the foot of the bed to pull myself to my feet, I stumble into the bathroom and reach for the pills beside the sink.

No pills. Using both my hands to feel all around the vanity in the darkened bathroom, I come up empty-handed.

A quick limp to the light switch illuminates the scene. My pain meds are nowhere to be found.

Checking the floor in case I accidentally knocked them off, I discover an empty amber canister in the trash. Shaking my head with befuddlement, I rub my eyes and do a double-take of the scene. I know I took a few pain pills, but I certainly didn't blow through an entire bottle.

And whether it's extrasensory perception or historical data, I know beyond a shadow of a doubt that my grandmother is to blame.

"Myrtle Isadora Johnson Linder Duncan Willamet Rogers. Show yourself this instant."

Of all the times for her to choose the slow, sparkly reentry—

"You've got to be kidding me."

"I'm not sure what you mean, dear. This is the reentry you told me you preferred."

"You're not wrong. Thing is, I have a bit of a situation on my hands and I'd like to address it as quickly as possible."

She paints her features as the portrait of innocence, and, once again, I know exactly where I got my acting skills.

"Now, Mitzy—"

"Save it, Isadora. What did you do with my pain medication?"

"Mitzy, you have a problem." She crosses her arms and avoids my question.

"Here we go again. Grams, I respect your struggle with alcohol, and I'm glad you found AA and turned your life around, but I'm not an alcoholic. And the actual problem I have is a badly sprained ankle. I need the pain medication because I'm in pain."

Walking faster than recommended for my healing ankle, I blast through her spectral form and flop onto the bed.

She swooshes after me and continues her lecture. "I hear what you're saying, sweetie, but I have more experience in this area than you do. You might not be an alcoholic, but you're a little too dependent on the pills." Her chin lifts defiantly.

"Grams, it's only been a few days. I wouldn't call that dependency."

"I'm sure you wouldn't, which is why I had to intervene. You were taking more than the prescribed dose, and sometimes you were taking them at shorter intervals than recommended as well. You absolutely know the medicine is interfering with your psychic abilities, and if you're honest with yourself, I don't think you're in that much pain."

My hands ball into fists at my side and I take several deep breaths to avoid saying something I'll regret. "To be clear, I'm an adult. I don't need a nursemaid. Now it's the middle of the night, my ankle is killing me, and I have no way to get back to sleep!"

The image of Ghost-ma flickers. "Is it killing you, really?"

Her tinge of remorse forces me to examine my situation more carefully. If I'm honest with myself, the pain isn't unbearable, but it's uncomfortable and inconvenient.

She hovers next to the bedside table and clicks her tongue. "Inconvenience doesn't require heavy-duty opioids, sweetie. The fact that you don't think you can get to sleep without the aid of your medication should be of more concern to you than it is."

I want to shout at her to get out of my head, but, in my mostly lucid state, some of what she's saying makes sense. The pills were an easy fix. When I numbed the pain, I could continue sleuthing my way around town on an ankle that should've been elevated with ice and rest, or whatever that crabby doctor said.

Grams arches an ethereal eyebrow and offers soft confirmation. "Mmhmm."

"Hey, let's not gloat. You may be right about me using the pills too freely, but that doesn't give you the right to judge the crap out of me in the middle of the night."

She bows gracefully. "Understood. Maybe you

could make yourself some hot chocolate and see if that will help you fall back to sleep. You and your foot could do with some additional rest. There'll be plenty of time to visit sweet young Quince tomorrow."

Exhaling with unnecessary force, I carefully swing my feet to the floor.

Crutch: check.

Hobble: check.

Ghost gloat: double check.

CHAPTER 16

AFTER THE HOT chocolate eases my transition to dreamland, I'm rewarded with several luscious dreamtime episodes starring Sheriff Too-Hot-To-Handle.

Morning comes too soon.

In an effort to prove my grandmother wrong, I choose to skip refilling my painkiller prescription. Instead, I wiggle into a fresh pair of yoga pants, a pullover hoodie sporting a picture of a naked cupcake with the tagline, "Sprinkles are for winners," and a beanie to cover my white haystack of hair. Adding a layer of the appropriate winter garments, I grab my crutch and hobble on down to breakfast-town—medication free.

I barely make it through the front door of Myrtle's Diner when Tatum accosts me. "Oh my gosh!

What happened to Quince?" Her eyes are wide, and my drug-free psychic senses get a blast of young-love panic.

Lifting one hand in a gesture that begs reprieve, I offer a compromise. "I tell you what, if you let me have a seat, and bring me a cup of coffee, I will absolutely tell you anything you want to know."

She bobs her head like the appropriately named dashboard doll and dives behind the counter.

Stretched out in a red-vinyl booth with my leg elevated on the seat next to me, I smile warmly as Tatum approaches with my cup of liquid alert. Her hand is shaking and a little go-go juice spills from the cup.

"Why don't you sit down?"

She slides into the booth and leans across the table eagerly.

I glance toward my grandfather behind the grill, and he subtly nods his approval.

Sneaking a quick sip, I launch into my tale. "Let me start by saying everything that happened was my fault, and I honestly wish I could trade places with Quince."

Tatum swallows audibly and sniffles. "Is he going to be okay?"

"I'm headed over to the hospital as soon as I finish breakfast. Erick assures me that Quince is young and invincible, if that counts for anything."

She nods, bites her lip, and blinks back tears. "I heard he was unconscious."

"Yeah, he got into a struggle with the suspected killer, and the guy shoved him into some shelving. Quince definitely hit his head. But I honestly don't think it's serious. I promise I'll update you as soon as I leave the hospital."

She draws a quick breath and bites her lip again. "Thanks. Here's my phone."

I type in my phone number and hand the cell back to her.

She immediately sends me a text. "That's me. You can text me, like, from the hospital if you want."

"Copy that."

A flash of relief relaxes her tense shoulders. "So he was fighting the guy?"

It's no skin off my nose to make the kid sound like a hero. "Totally. We had put a few pieces of the puzzle together and it was really starting to look like the guy was the murderer, and Quince ran back to make sure he didn't tamper with evidence. By the time I got there, your boy Quince was all over him!"

Her cheeks flush, and she smiles proudly. "He's, like, the best, you know?"

Taking a big sip of coffee and letting her savor the moment, I nod my agreement. "He really is."

Odell approaches with my breakfast, and

Tatum scoots out of the booth and casts her guilty eyes toward the floor.

"So, is your secret crush gonna live to tell the tale?"

Tatum looks up with eyes as wide as saucers. "Huh?"

Odell's gruff chuckle warms my heart, and I answer for her. "Quince is gonna be great. I just wish there was someone to run a story about him in the paper. The hometown hero, you know what I mean?"

He slides my scrambled eggs with chorizo onto the table and follows it with a bottle of Tabasco. "I know exactly what you mean." Odell winks at me and returns to the kitchen.

Tatum busies herself wiping down tables and refilling sugar shakers.

Once I finish my scrumptious meal, I balance on my crutch and scoop up my dishes. It's a little precarious and I'm wondering if I'm going to make it safely to the dish bin when a familiar voice interrupts my progress.

"Let me help you with that, Moon." Sheriff Harper snags the dishes from my hand and deposits them in the bus bin behind the counter. "Can I offer you a ride to the hospital?"

My mouth hangs open like a broken shutter on a haunted house, and, before I can regain my composure, I witness a sly wink exchanged between my boyfriend and my grandfather.

I don't know how Odell managed to cook and send a text, but I do not like it when these two work together. I do not like it one bit. "Yes, I graciously accept your offer, Sheriff." Glancing over my shoulder at Odell, I narrow my gaze and shake my head.

He pretends to ignore my nonverbal warning and scrapes away at his grill.

Erick helps me out to the patrol car parked at the curb and heads toward the Birch County Regional Medical Facility.

"Have you heard anything? He's going to be all right, isn't he?"

"They put a couple of stitches in the cut on his head, but nothing was fractured, and there's no serious internal bleeding. They're going to release him later today, and the doctor told me there shouldn't be any complications."

"Thank goodness! I still feel terrible—"

"Don't beat yourself up, Moon. The kid's quick thinking protected the evidence. I wish he hadn't gotten hurt, but I'm grateful Oscar wasn't able to cover his tracks."

"Yeah, about that. Have you questioned him?"

Erick nods. "Yeah, we got a few answers out of him before he demanded a lawyer."

"Bummer. Anything useful?"

He shrugs. "Honestly? I don't think so. He tried to put the blame on Herman Pettit. Makes no sense to me."

I ponder the tactic. "Yeah, that's a little odd. I mean, Herman didn't exactly like Quade, but he didn't know his routine. He couldn't have known that Quade would—"

"Well, we're bringing Herman in for questioning. So, we'll find out exactly what he knows."

My eyes light up and I offer the sheriff my best sexy smile. "Any chance I might get front row seats to that?"

He grins wickedly, walks two fingers across the seat and turns up his palm as he says, "I'm not sure you can afford tickets."

My skin tingles all over, and I know there's a blush creeping up my cheeks. "You underestimate the value of my estate, Sheriff. I'm willing to pay whatever it takes."

Direct hit!

Erick's tender blue eyes widen, and he leans toward his door with a sharp intake of breath. "Whoa. I forgot who I was dealing with."

I slide my hand into his and wink. "See that it doesn't happen again."

We park near the entrance to the large hospital, and he instructs me to sit tight and wait for assistance. Even though I have some personal issues with the phrase "sit tight," I do as I'm told.

He comes around to my side of the vehicle and gallantly helps me extract myself and my crutch from the cruiser.

As we pass through the sliding doors at the main entrance, he tips his head in that way that insinuates he's doffing a cap, and the stern woman at the reception desk startles and smiles broadly. Traveling with a sheriff's escort seems to be just the ticket.

The elder Knudsen, or, as I've recently learned, Quintin, is posted up next to his son's bed. His features are pinched, and the second we walk into the room, I feel his nerves flare. His brother was recently murdered, and now his son attacked . . . I can hardly blame the man for being a little jumpy.

Quince sees me and beams. "Did you get the evidence?"

I grin and tilt my head toward Erick. "The sheriff said you done good."

The young man's smile widens, nearly splitting his face in two, and he nods. "Sweet."

"Unfortunately, as Deputy Paulsen would say, he lawyered up, as the guilty always do."

Quince's smile fades, but before he can comment, his father jumps in with an unrequested explanation. "It's an unfortunate side effect of the legal system that criminals are often offered more protection than their victims. Seems to me that this Oscar Wiggins was caught red-handed. I am sure the founding fathers didn't imagine protecting murderers when they carefully crafted our country's constitution. However, the climate in the 1700s was vastly different from where we find ourselves—"

Sheriff Harper to the rescue. "Don't worry, Quintin. We'll file the necessary paperwork and get the information we need. Your son did the department a huge favor by locating that evidence and protecting the crime scene. Of course, we'll need him to come down to make a full statement when he's feeling better."

Quintin smiles, and his massive frog-like eyes blink several times behind his thick glasses.

A sudden flash of heat around my ring finger makes my heart jump. *Please don't be bad news*, I silently hope as I glance at the misty black dome.

The ring shows me an adorable picture of Tatum holding a milkshake. Aha! Now's my chance. "Hey, did I mention Tatum was totally worried about you? I'll let her know you're all right."

The normally monosyllabic Quince smiles eagerly. "She was? Sweet. Yeah, tell her I'm, like, gonna be fine. I'll come down to the diner to tell all about the fight and stuff."

Arching one of my eyebrows, I smile and nod. "Sure, I'll tell her that."

The intensity of my gaze brings a slight flush to his cheeks, and he looks away self-consciously.

"You should take her ice-skating to celebrate. I heard something about the hockey arena being open for free skate on Sunday afternoons."

His Adam's apple bobs ferociously, and my extra senses pick up on his nervous anticipation.

"In case you were wondering, Quince, she'll say yes."

He smiles adorably and jerks his head to flick his bangs back without thinking. "Ahhh! Dude. My head."

"Yeah, you might want to take it easy on the head flicks for a few days."

Chuckles ripple through the crowd, and Quince shrugs. "I'll try, dude."

"Glad you're okay, *dude*. Me and the sheriff better head out and wrap up this case."

I offer a single nod to the elder Knudsen and crutch on out.

Erick suffers from a severe case of good manners and gets involved in a rather lengthy verbal exchange before he catches up to me.

"I can't believe you let yourself get sucked into a conversation with Quintin! That man is a walking Wikipedia rabbit hole."

The sheriff lifts one shoulder and smiles. "Hey, a voter is a voter. I have to win votes wherever I can."

The smile fades from my face as the harsh taste of reality hits me full force. "Oh, right? I totally forgot you're an elected official."

He opens my door for me and grins. "Yeah, that tracks. Maybe now that you've had a little reminder, you can keep your eavesdropping shenanigans on the down low."

"Absolutely, Sheriff. Whatever I can do to support your campaign."

His shoulders shake with laughter as he circles around the front of the vehicle to the driver's door.

Back at the quaint little sheriff's station that I still think of as a cross between Sheriff Valenti's office in *Roswell* and good old-fashioned Sheriff Andy Taylor's digs in *Mayberry*, Erick escorts me into his office.

Deputy Gilbert pokes his head in. "Pettit is in two, Sheriff."

"10-4."

Erick stands and rifles through some files on his desk. Eventually, he settles on a thin manila folder and adds a few stray photographs to the file. "Enjoy the ambience of my *office*, Moon."

"10-4."

He shakes his head and crosses the hallway into Interrogation Room 2.

As soon as the latch clicks, I get my one-gal, three-legged race into motion and crutch it into the observation room. When I ease open the door, shock barely begins to describe the emotion that hits me.

"What do you think you're doing in here, Moon?" Deputy Paulsen occupies the one and only chair, and she has a large piece of what I can only assume is wild game-based jerky in her hand. This assumption rests solely on smell—which ain't great.

"Oh, I thought this was the bathroom."

She scoffs openly. "This room is for official sheriff's personnel only. You can wait in his office."

I toy with the idea of bandying my confidential informant status about, but I'm fairly certain that won't get me anywhere with Paulsen. "Sure, I'll do that."

Clumsily rotating my operation, I exit the observation room.

Dagnabbit! I need to hear that interview.

If at first you don't succeed, try, try again.

Taking a deep breath, I grab the handle on the door of the occupied interrogation room and stumble my way in.

Erick looks up in frustration. "Can we help you, Miss Moon?"

I smile and shrug. "I was hoping I could help you. Deputy Gilbert mentioned that Mr. Pettit was in this room. Since I'd promised him I would look into those cow incidents . . . I thought maybe this thing was about that."

The sheriff exhales through his teeth and gestures toward a chair. "It hasn't come up yet, but it might."

As I take my seat beside Herman Pettit, the smell of mustache wax and tobacco pricks a memory I can't quite grasp. "Do you smoke, Mr. Pettit?"

Erick opens his mouth to protest my interference, but Herman Pettit shakes his head and moves to answer. "No, no. Why do you ask?"

"I smell tobacco. Isn't that weird?"

He grips the edge of the table with his thick hands and chuckles. "Actually, it's not that strange." He gently strokes his tightly curved red handlebar mustache, and adds, "The mustache wax I use is tobacco and leather scented. It's nice, don't you think?"

"It is. Where do you get something like that?"

The seemingly innocent question brings a strange response from Herman. He swallows audibly and crosses his arms.

Odd.

He shifts in his chair and mumbles, "Oh, it was a gift."

"Wow. How nice." I smile and nod for Erick to continue his interview.

He sighs and attempts to maintain his professionalism. "Mr. Pettit, have you—"

"Ah ha!" I jolt to my feet and my crutch hits the ground with a clang.

"Miss Moon, please control yourself." Erick leans back and gazes at me with concern.

As I slip from my mind movie back into reality, I attempt to cover my outburst with a weak chuckle and a weaker lie. "Sorry, I just remembered I have an appointment." Stooping, I collect my crutch and head for the door. "If you'll excuse me."

Both men are left in my wake with their eyes wide and their jaws flapping in the breeze.

CHAPTER 17

My KNOWLEDGE of Deputy Paulsen's whereabouts now seems beyond serendipitous. I approach the innocent and impressionable Deputy Gilbert. "Hey, I need to ask Mr. Wiggins a quick question. Is it all right if I head back to the cells?"

He looks around the bullpen for a superior officer, and finding none makes the executive decision to help me out. "Sure, I guess. You're not planning on staying in there long, are you?"

I widen my eyes and smile. "Oh, of course not. I never push my luck."

Regardless of the fact that this answer is one hundred percent falsehood, it offers the deputy the reassurance he requires.

"Follow me."

He grabs a set of keys from a hook on the wall

inside Erick's office, and I grow concerned that he may have misunderstood. "Oh, I don't need to go in the cell. I just need to ask a question."

"Yeah, I got that. We installed a new security door. Sheriff Harper is putting in some security upgrades prior to the city council's inspection."

Security upgrades? City council inspections? I can't even! Just when I'd fooled myself into thinking that I knew everything there was to know about Erick's life. "Gosh, that sounds like a lot of bureaucratic nonsense."

Deputy Gilbert smirks and leans toward me as he whispers. "The old salts on the force say this kinda stuff happens every four years, but, between you and me, I'd call it polishing a turd."

The phrase accurately describes pretty much my exact thoughts about the station's interior design, and I laugh too easily. "Right? I'd sooner see a little money go toward a computer or two, before I worried about a security door protecting a few cells that are usually standing empty."

He smiles, but shifts to a more serious tone. "Don't let the small town fool you. The cells have occupants more often than most of our residents realize."

"Point taken. I appreciate you escorting me back."

He nods as he unlocks the new security door.

"Yeah, I'll have to stay. Procedure, you know?"

"Oh, sure. No problem."

Deputy Gilbert double-checks that the heavily riveted metal security door closes behind us and motions for me to continue to the cell while he remains by the hatch.

He's a thoughtful guy. I honestly hope he doesn't get into trouble for letting me back here.

As I approach Oscar Wiggins' cell, he jumps to his feet. "Are you gonna let me outta here? I didn't kill anybody. I swear."

"Hi, Mr. Wiggins." I wiggle my fingers in a halfhearted greeting.

He takes one look at my hair and my crutch and shakes his head. "You? I got nothing to say to you."

"Look, I'm not here to make any accusations. I hope you're as innocent as you say. I only have one question."

He crosses his arms and stares at me with beady, uncooperative eyes.

I need him to walk just a little closer. Whispering nonsense under my breath, I glance toward him for a response.

"What?" He shakes his head and scoffs.

I whisper additional nonsense, but enunciate the words *freedom* and *innocence*. That one draws him in.

He takes two steps closer to the bars. "I can't

hear you. If you came back here to ask me something, you might as well speak up."

Leaning forward, I inhale deeply and smile. I
knew I'd smelled it somewhere before! "Where do
you get your mustache wax, Mr. Wiggins?"

He steps back and smooths his sharply trimmed
dark mustache with the side of one finger. "My
mustache wax? I don't get it anywhere. My wife
makes it."

All sorts of psychic bells and whistles are going
off in my head.

Mr. Pettit and Mr. Wiggins, who are technically sworn enemies, just happen to use the same
mustache wax? I think not. "Your wife, Tammy,
makes mustache wax?"

For some reason, this topic pierces his veil of
sworn silence. "Sure. Sure. She makes all kinds of
grooming products for men. She said my scruffy
beard and unruly mustache were her inspiration."
He lifts his chin proudly and smiles.

"Well, it looks great. Whatever she puts in that
stuff is magic."

His genuine smile crinkles the corners of his
eyes. "She's really talented. The house is a disaster
area, though. She's like a mad scientist, but I think
things are finally gonna turn around for us."

"Turn around? Have you been having relationship troubles?"

His jaw tenses, and his goatee seems to flinch. "I think I'm done talking to you."

"Understood." I nod politely and hobble back toward the waiting deputy.

Deputy Gilbert unlocks the security door and holds it for me. "Did you get the answer you needed?"

"I sure did. Thanks for your help."

Lucky for both of us, I make it back to Erick's office, and Gilbert replaces the key, before the sheriff exits the interrogation room.

When Erick returns to his office, I'm grinning like the cat that swallowed the canary.

"That look concerns me, Moon."

He leans back in his chair, and part of me feels that he's crossed his arms in a purposeful attempt to distract me.

"I may have found the break in the case you've been waiting for, Sheriff."

Erick stretches his arms up and laces his fingers together behind his head. My eyes dart down and his deep, throaty chuckle makes my skin tingle. "Save your rewards for later. What have you got?"

I'd love to say I have a case of heart palpitations and possibly mild heat stroke, but I'm not about to let him get the upper hand. "Did you know that Tammy Wiggins makes men's grooming products?"

"I think you mean Tammy Smythe-Wiggins."

His smug grin is the last straw.

"Whatever her name is, she makes a tobacco-and-leather-scented mustache wax."

His arms fall to his sides, and he leans forward. "The product used by Herman Pettit?"

"The very one. It's also used by her husband. Which would indicate she has a personal fondness for the scent. I can only think of one reason why Herman Pettit would be using the same scented mustache wax as her husband."

Erick takes a deep breath and shouts. "Deputy Gilbert, get in here."

Gilbert darkens the door with a face full of regret. "Well, she's your girlfriend, sir."

Erick's expression shifts to concerned confusion. He glances at me and shakes his head. "I don't even want to know. Bring in Tammy Smythe-Wiggins. Code 3."

"10-4." Deputy Gilbert wastes no time in sprinting toward his vehicle.

The sheriff gestures at the departing deputy and frowns. "I'd appreciate it if you'd resist using your feminine wiles on my staff."

The unintentional double entendre makes me giggle and blush. Words escape, but I manage to choke out an "Mmhmm."

He blushes but maintains his stern visage.

"Um, I need to get back to the bookshop. Call

me when Tammy gets here?"

He stands, saunters across his office, and threads an arm between my crutch and my body as he squeezes my waist. "Just making sure I have your vote in the upcoming election, Miss Moon."

Erick's nearness and serious tone send me into another giggle fit. "You kidding? I'm not even registered to vote in Birch County."

He pulls away and crosses his arms. "Democracy is the cornerstone of civilization. I'm not sure I can date a girl who doesn't vote."

The matter-of-fact statement catches me off guard. I stumble backward in shock.

My chivalrous boyfriend can simultaneously save me and stand for his principles. As he catches my elbow and pulls me close, he whispers, "The election isn't until November. You've got plenty of time to get registered."

"Copy that."

He kisses me softly on the lips, and I shamble back to the bookstore in a fog, shouldering a combination of bliss and consternation.

As soon as I make it through the intricately carved front door, I shout, "Grams! Grams, I need to talk to you!"

The distinct sound of biker boots stomps from the back room, and Twiggy gestures down the historical fiction aisle where an actual customer must be browsing. "I've told you a thousand times, call me Twiggy. 'Grams' makes me feel old."

My skin flushes with embarrassment as I realize Twiggy's generous effort to cover my faux pas. "Sorry, Twiggy. That's the last time. I promise."

She crosses her arms and rolls her eyes, indicating she's not falling for my pseudo-promises for one minute.

However, she actually takes pity on me and unhooks the chain so I can stumble up the wrought-iron circular staircase with one less obstacle.

"Thanks."

"Don't get used to it, doll."

Classic Twiggy. I grab the candle handle next to my copy of *Saducismus Triumphatus* and wait impatiently for the bookcase door to slide open. Once inside, the intense throbbing of my ankle reminds me of my desire to prove my grandmother wrong. I flop onto the overstuffed settee and elevate my aching leg.

Grams floats absently from the closet and startles into a freeze-frame when she sees me. "I didn't hear you come in."

"Wow. You must've been planning quite an outfit. Dare I ask?"

A strange melancholy seeps from her flickering aura, and she drifts toward me without purpose.

"Grams, what's wrong?"

"What, dear?"

"You seem like you're a million miles away. What's on your mind?"

"I was wondering if the last time I wore the Vivienne Westwood trench was with Odell?"

"The missing coat? The one the cleaners lost? Did you remember something?"

Her head tilts oddly, and she runs her tongue across her shimmering teeth. "Didn't I tell you?"

"Um, no. That would be why I don't know, and why I'm asking."

"Of course, dear. I understand."

I lift my hands in the air and nod encouragingly.

She smiles wistfully and hovers above the scalloped-back chair. "I thought maybe Odell might remember something, so I mentioned it to him the last time we were chatting."

"And?"

"Well, he said all coats look the same to him, but I told him to donate a few things to the library's charity auction before I passed away. That obviously sounds like something I'd do, right?"

"Yes, it does. So now we solved the mystery. The matter is closed?"

"Not exactly."

"Dear Lord baby Jesus, Isadora. If I'm going to have to drag everything out of you as though you were Quince Knudsen, I'll lose my mind. Just tell me the whole story. All at once. No stops." Whew! The lack of pain medication is definitely getting to me.

She crosses her arms and taps her coral lip with a perfectly manicured finger. "You don't say."

I narrow my gaze and glower in her general direction.

"Fine, fine. I'll get on with it. Dear, sweet, Odell said when we first met—"

"Yeesh! I don't need that much backstory!"

"Let me finish, young lady."

Taking a pantomime from her repertoire, I grab an invisible key from the air, lock my lips, and stuff it down my shirt.

"You're such a hoot. Anyway, Odell said he would call the library to see if they had a record of the items I donated."

"Great googly moogly! What does that have to do with 'when you first met'?" I'm beginning to think this coat is her "Rosebud." Classic *Citizen Kane* callback. The clever idea brings a smile to my lips.

"It's not that clever, sweetie."

I point my fingers at my lips and shake my head.

"Let it go, dear. The point of the story is Odell's generosity."

All of my resistance melts away like an ice cube

left on the counter. "You're right, Grams! That's absolutely the sweetest thing. It's nice to know I'm not the only one who's here for you."

She zooms down to eye level, and her ghostly irises are sparkling. "Isn't it just?"

"Seems like you're positively giddy. What are you really up to?"

Grams presses a hand to her bosom and widens her eyes. "I'm not up to anything. Odell mentioned how he'll visit me every day after you and Erick get married—"

"All of you need to stop this nonsense. I am not getting married." Once the words pass through my lips, a strange sensation washes over me. Erick and Odell are quite close. It's entirely possible that Odell knows something I don't, despite my psychic gifts.

"That's exactly what I was thinking, sweetie."

I point my fingers at my lips and shake my head.

"Oh Mitzy, let it go. Odell said once you and Erick are married, you'll want a place for yourselves. Erick lives with his mother, you live with your ghost mother, and having a clean slate to build whatever you want, seems like the perfect plan."

"IF I get married, I'll cross that bridge when I come to it." I lift my left hand and wiggle my fingers. "The only thing missing from this perfect arrangement . . ."

She glances at the antique mood ring and frowns. "Well, you'll just have to switch that to your right hand."

"I don't think I can."

"What do you mean? Is it stuck?" She reaches a glimmering hand toward my ring finger.

"Not physically. But psychically, I think that's where it has to be."

"You've never tried it on your right hand, dear. How would you know?"

Crossing my arms, I tilt my head and arch an eyebrow. "Between the two of us, which one is a living psychic?"

She opens her mouth to protest, but instead sighs dramatically. "That's not fair. I have the occasional vision."

"I accept that. And I'm not trying to brag, but even by Silas's standards, I have exceptional gifts. If I say the moody mood ring stays on the left hand, then that's where it stays. Deal?"

Ghost-ma throws her glowing limbs in the air. "Fine. I'll tell th—" She slaps a ring-ensconced hand over her mouth.

"You'll tell who, what?" My heart races, and I can't be sure if it's panic or excitement.

Grams pulls the old disappearing ghost trick, and my opportunity to interrogate her further vanishes.

CHAPTER 18

I MAY HAVE STORMED out of the apartment in a huff after Grams ducked out on our conversation, but as soon as I reach the top of the spiral staircase, my mood ring flashes an image of the chain.

Twiggy!

Heading to the back room, I run through possible scenarios to entice my stubborn employee to take my side.

"Hey, do you have a minute?"

Twiggy slowly rotates her dilapidated office chair toward me as though she's the captain of a starship, and I've interrupted her daily log. Her expression makes it clear that I have seconds, not minutes, to make my case.

"Look, I'll be quick. Grams was asking me a lot of weird, ring-related questions and then she almost let something slip about telling 'them.' Somebody better tell me what's going on!"

Twiggy lifts her foot and places one biker boot on the opposite knee of her dungarees. "Or what, kid?"

"Or . . ." She has a point. My threat is beyond empty. "I don't know. I got nothin'. The point is, I hate surprises. It's a long story that starts with my mother's unfortunate death, and, despite all the fantastic things that have happened to me in the last few years, I'm still not a fan. No matter what, I can't stand being surprised. I'm a passable actress, though. So if you give me some idea what's going on, I promise I'll act surprised."

Twiggy rewards me with a knee slapping. "I told those fools it was pointless to try to surprise the psychic!" She continues to laugh uproariously at my expense.

"So there is a surprise. Dish."

She tilts her head and savors the moment. I'm utterly at her mercy, and she's enjoying it way too much. "Tell you what. I'll give you the broad strokes, and then you keep your snoopy little nose to yourself. Not all surprises are bad."

It sounds like the best, and probably only, deal I'm likely to receive. "You have my word."

The response seems to satisfy her, and she nods her head as she begins the tale. "I'd say your grandmother is the instigator, but she ropes more folks into her production with each passing day."

"My grandmother? She was super focused on something about a ring. I hope Erick's not trying to set up a secret proposal at my birthday party."

Twiggy lifts both hands in the air and stares me down. "Would that really be so bad?"

"That's not the point. I don't want to get into it. Just tell me more stuff about Grams and her production."

"Well, I suppose Isadora had a bit of a guilty conscience. Those first few months you were here, she didn't know when your birthday was. The second year she was trapped in that cursed piece of jewelry. So, this year she's bound and determined to make your twenty-fourth birthday one for the record books."

Even though the thought of a massive gala terrifies me, a whisper of relief spreads throughout my body. "Is that all? She just wants to plan some ridiculously elaborate birthday party?"

Twiggy rotates her chair, opens the drawer under the built-in desk, and pulls out a thick stack of pages. "It started with once a week, but now I find a new to-do list, scratched out in creepy ghost handwriting, on my desk every day. Decorations, catering, musicians, guest lists, valets . . . Isadora seems hell-bent on breaking the bank."

Leaning on my crutch, I chuckle and catch my breath. "I'm sure I'll hate every minute of it, but it makes me happy to make her happy. I let go of special days and big parties a long time ago, but my dad and Amaryllis had a pretty fantastic wedding here, so I suppose having a comically over-the-top birthday party at the bookstore will at least be a fraction of fun."

She slaps her hand on her thigh. "That's the spirit, doll. Whoever said your birthday party should be about you is dead wrong."

We share a snicker at Grams' expense.

"So who's involved in this crazy plotting and planning? I don't want to put anyone on the spot unnecessarily. I know Grams has probably threatened to haunt anyone who breaks the rules."

Twiggy's dark eyes widen. "Did she say that? If you somehow got me cursed, you'll never hear the end of it, kid."

"Don't worry, she's not around."

Twiggy checks her arms for ghost chills, leans forward, and continues in a whisper. "All the usual suspects. Odell, your dad, Amaryllis, Stellen, Erick, me—"

"Erick? How did Erick get into the inner circle?"

"Well, I had to tell him what the permits were for."

I nearly drop my crutch. "Permits? This party is gonna be so big there are permits?"

Twiggy enjoys one more cackle. "She wants to close off the cul-de-sac for the band, and she's got a bonfire planned as well, weather permitting."

Shock grips me. "Weather permitting indeed! If this coming March is anything like the last one, the cul-de-sac will be under six feet of snow!"

Twiggy sighs and rubs her hand across her mouth wistfully. "I learned a long time ago not to argue with your grandmother. What Isadora wants, Isadora gets. If she could figure out a way to hold a wedding reception outside in December, she'll manage to have a birthday party anywhere she wants any time of the year."

I have to laugh. "You're not wrong."

She drops both feet to the floor and exhales. "Well, let's see your surprised face, doll."

I grip my crutch with one hand, open my eyes as wide as saucers, and press one hand to my chest as I gasp. "Oh, my gosh!"

Twiggy gives me a slow clap as she turns back toward our antique computer.

As I head out into the stacks, I shout a "thanks" over my shoulder.

Hmmm, I can't believe I haven't heard from Erick. Deputy Gilbert should absolutely be back with Tammy by now.

Grabbing my cell, I fire off a quick text.

PING.

"He came back empty-handed."

My first instinct is to run upstairs and grab the map, and the pendulum, and scry for her location—but luckily my restored extrasensory perceptions reward me with a clairaudient message before I have to struggle with the stairs.

Herman Pettit.

I want to hear the happiness in Erick's voice when I give him the news, so this time I choose to place a call. As soon as he answers, I blurt, "She went straight to Herman Pettit's. I'll bet you any-thing they're packing their bags and getting ready to make a run for it."

At least he thanks me before he abruptly hangs up.

Now we wait.

I don't remember Twiggy mentioning Silas on the list of Isadora's birthday accomplices. I need to call him and see if he has any ideas for pain man-agement. It's come to my attention that my grand-mother was absolutely right about the way the pain medication was affecting me. I can't take a chance on refilling that prescription and poten-tially taking the easy way out too often or too many times.

For some reason, the children's section beckons

me. I teeter as I lower myself onto a large bright-green beanbag chair without incident.

Placing a call on speaker, I reach out to Silas. He answers on the second ring.

"Good afternoon, Mizithra. How are you recovering?"

And he keeps trying to convince me he's not psychic. "Interesting you should mention my recovery. I'm having some difficulties."

Ignoring my failure to follow the proper greeting protocol, he continues. "That seems burdensome. How may I assist you?"

"I was wondering if you knew some type of spell, I mean, transmutation, to reduce pain?"

"Did the doctor not prescribe some type of medication to assist in pain management?"

"Um, yeah, she did. The problem is, I had a little trouble monitoring my dosages."

"Addiction?"

"No, Grams intervened before it could get too serious, but, I have to admit, the substance was interfering with my powers. The problem is, she flushed all my pills down the toilet, and now my ankle hurts like a—"

"Language, Mizithra."

"What? I was going to say like a tight pair of pants on Thanksgiving."

The hearty sound of his laughter is reward enough.

"So, have you got anything up your sleeve, or in that magical tweed coat of yours?"

The depth of his concern is clear in that he doesn't take the time to correct my use of the word magical. "There are two transmutations that may assist. I should have time for a short tutorial en route to the airport."

"What now? Did you say airport?"

"Indeed. Earlier today, I received some unfortunate news. My brother Jedediah has been unwell, as you know. However, his nurse reached out this morning and informed me he has taken a dark turn. They do not expect him to recover. I chose to fly rather than waste precious time on a train. End-of-life predictions are notoriously unreliable. I may have a few days with my brother, or perhaps a few months. Either way, I put my affairs in order and have arranged to stay with him till he crosses over."

The discussion of a close relative passing threatens to loosen the manhole cover keeping all of my feelings about my mother's death at bay. "I'm so sorry, Silas. I know you and your brother are close, and I'm sure this must be difficult for you."

"When one reaches my age, or that of my older sibling, certain facts of life are inevitable. Jedediah has lived a full life. He will be missed, but neither he nor I have regrets."

"I wish I had that kind of clarity about death."

"One day, it will find you. Meanwhile, live each day to its fullest." His voice catches, and he covers it with a brusque harrumph.

"I'll try. We will miss you in Pin Cherry, but I completely understand. I promise to stay out of trouble while you're away."

And, for the second time during this phone call, I receive surprising guffaws for my outstanding remarks.

"Rude. I can stay out of trouble, most of the time."

His wise voice says otherwise. "I have come to understand that you would not be yourself without your penchant for mischief. Acceptance is one of the greatest gifts one can give oneself. I am pleased with the progress you have made with your gifts and your alchemical studies. I shall not beat my brow against the mountain in a fruitless attempt to change your nature."

"Thanks, I think."

"You are welcome. It was indeed meant as a compliment. I shall be on my way shortly and should see you before the hour."

Before I have a chance to express my gratitude,

Pyewacket darts out of the shadows and scrapes his deadly claws along the side of the beanbag chair.

"Pyewacket! You spilled the beans everywhere!"

A concerned voice echoes from the speaker on my mobile phone. "Mitzy? Are you injured?"

"No, I'll live. It's just that I was actually sort of comfortable, in this huge beanbag chair in the children's book section, and Pyewacket came out of nowhere and ripped the side open with his razor claws!"

Silas harrumphs into the phone, and I can easily picture him smoothing his mustache with thumb and forefinger. "Interesting. Perhaps there is a deeper meaning."

"The only thing deep about it is my rear end sinking deep into the middle of this stupid chair! There's absolutely no way I'm going to be able to get out of here on my own."

Silas attempts to stifle a chuckle. "Fear not. Elevate your leg, see if you can pry any additional details from Robin Pyewacket Goodfellow, and I shall see you posthaste."

CHAPTER 19

DESPITE THE ENCOURAGEMENT from my mentor, Pyewacket offers no additional explanation for his actions. Instead, he lies atop the low two-shelf bookcase filled with colorful early reader books and squeezes his eyes to slits. Meanwhile, the beans continue to ooze from the wound he caused. I've never been trapped in quicksand, although I've seen many a movie that featured that classic scene, but I assume there's a similar sinking sensation with a potentially more terrifying outcome.

In my case, each passing minute sinks me further into a compromising position. Not compromising in a tawdry way, compromising in the sense that no amount of compromise will ever again get me on my feet. I could call for Twiggy, but the thought of her discovering me in this predicament brings me no pleasure. Plus, I'm sure she would cackle herself near to death before she offered me any assistance.

As my backside sinks lower, my foot ends up somewhat elevated. Last night's lack of sleep officially catches up with me, and my heavy eyelids fall like the curtains at the end of a Broadway show.

"Mizithra, it seems you have already uncovered the secret of relaxation."

Blinking in confusion, I swipe at the drool trickling from the corner of my mouth and yawn loudly.

Silas covers his mouth politely as he yawns in response.

Looking up at the wizened alchemist, I chuckle. "Good news, Silas, you're not a psychopath."

He tugs at his bowtie and harrumphs. "I should think not. What on earth is the catalyst for such a declaration?"

"Ah, forget about it. It's just a stupid movie trope about how psychopaths, or maybe it's sociopaths, won't yawn in response if they see someone else yawn. It's something to do with their lack of empathy or— I don't know. I'm babbling. Can you help me out of this thing?"

"All in due time. Did you deduce Pyewacket's message?"

"Deduce his message? What I deduced is that

he's a spoiled brat, and he thought it would be hilarious to trap me in this chair. Was there more?"

Silas smooths his mustache with more agitation than I've previously witnessed. "I fear it is worse than your grandmother believed."

"What's worse?"

"This misplaced anger results from your rapid development of a dependence on the pain medication. But we'll get to that in a moment. On the phone, you made an exclamation about spilling the beans. What is it that you feel Pyewacket revealed?"

I have to bite my tongue. I'd love to make an incredibly snarky response and gesture to the pile of *revealed* beans on the floor, but one stern lecture from Mr. Willoughby is enough on this day. "I don't think there was a message, Silas. It was when I was about to call you . . . I felt drawn toward the children's section, and I sat in the beanbag chair. The next thing you know"—I gesture to the rip and pile of stuffing innards—"this happened."

He tugs on the lapels of his fusty tweed coat and ponders my report. "Drawn to the children's section, you say?"

"That's what I said."

He steeples his fingers and begins to bounce his chin on the tip of his pointers.

Oh boy. The lesson has begun, and I'm

coming up empty. "Children. Beans. I don't know. Spilling the beans on children?" I lift my hands in an "I give up" gesture, and, with a resounding mental "click," the pieces fall into place like the tiles in a master's game of Tetris. "Somebody spilled the beans about a child! This isn't the first 'child' clue either. When I was at the church, I touched one of the pews and the word 'child' popped into my head. Is there a secret about a kid, Pyewacket?"

"Reow." Can confirm.

Silas grins with an almost fatherly pride. "Well done, Mizithra. Now let us address your pain management." He reaches for a small chair and struggles to sit comfortably on the minuscule seat.

As comical as it is to watch him adjust his round belly and his large coat, I dare not chuckle.

Finally, he gets situated. "The thing about pain is that it exists most acutely in the mind."

"That doesn't sound totally true. When I sprained my ankle, it actually hurt. I didn't imagine it hurt."

"Certainly. Your point is valid. However, my point is that pain is relative."

I cross my arms and grumble. "I'm *relatively* sure I'm in pain."

He ignores my response. "Give me your hand."

"Finally." I reach out my hand, thinking that

he's going to hoist me out of my bright-green prison, but I'm completely wrong.

Silas pinches the skin on the back of my hand, and I yank it back with a yelp. "Ouch. That stings."

"Did it hurt more or less than your ankle?"

"Well, I'm not sure. I wasn't thinking about my ankle. I was thinking about how much my hand hurt."

He nods as though he's made an amazing point. "Exactly."

"What do you mean? You can't just say *exactly* and think that's a—" Oh, wait! He can. Because before I even finish my sentence, I understand exactly what he means. "I get it. When I sit and focus on the pain in my ankle, and give it all of my attention, it hurts quite a lot. However, when I'm distracted by sleuthing or hand pinching, it doesn't hurt nearly as much."

Silas nods. "Excellent. Now the key is to discover the thing that will consume your attention, distract you completely from your pain."

Without even trying, the first thing that pops into my mind is Erick. "I think I've got something."

He chuckles knowingly. "I assume you do. When the pain is getting the better of you, you must quiet your mind. Visualize a bubble of white light—"

"Like the Good Witch from Oz?"

Silas stares at me with utter disappointment. "I don't follow."

"Glinda, the Good Witch, travels in a— Never mind. Not what you meant. I'm listening. Please continue."

He harrumphs, but moves on. "Visualize the pain leaving your body and entering the bubble. Release the ball of light holding the pain and allow your mind to drift toward this alternate thing that holds your rapt attention. If your focus falters, gently pull it back. When combined properly, the bubble of light and the shift of focus will release you from the prison of pain. The more you practice, the more adept you will become."

"Can I use the bubble for other things? Could I offer to put someone else's pain in the bubble?"

His eyes shimmer with emotion. "It is so like you to think of others in this way. When we first met, I never imagined your heart housed such generosity. To answer your question, I have witnessed a man so fully relieve the pain of a patient that the surgeon was able to perform an operation in the field without anesthesia."

My inner sense of knowing hardly needs to ask the question, but my outer snoop must. "Was the man who removed the pain you?"

He casts his eyes downward. "One has no need to seek acclaim for one's actions. A selfless gesture is far more effective when the giver expects no reward."

"Understood. I hope you can take away some of your brother's pain. I know that's why you're going."

A ready tear trickles over his round cheek and down his droopy jowl. "Indeed. If it is within my power to ease my brother's passing, I will offer my assistance without hesitation."

Grabbing my crutch, I awkwardly shove myself towards Silas. He reaches out and catches me as I struggle to embrace him. "I'll never understand what Fates conspired to bring you and me together, Mr. Willoughby, but I'm grateful, and my life will never be the same."

"Nor will mine, Mizithra Achelois Moon."

"Ree-oow." A rarely heard intonation from our feline overlord, but it seems to indicate conspiratorial agreement.

My phone pings with a text notification as I'm escorting Silas to the front door. It's easy to guess that the message is likely from Sheriff Harper, but after the tender moment Mr. Willoughby and I exchanged, I don't dare check my phone in front of him and break etiquette.

He turns, smooths his mustache with thumb and forefinger, and smiles warmly. "May I drop you at the sheriff's station?"

Despite my newfound pain management transmutation, the thought of poking my way through the snow and ice for a couple blocks does little to entice me. "That would be—"

"Divine?" Silas winks.

"Exactly. Let me grab my coat."

At the curb, Silas protests as I offer him one last overzealous hug before exiting his ancient automobile.

He putters away, and I enter the sheriff's station filled with hope and brimming with secrets.

Erick instantly walks out of his office as though a hidden production assistant cued him from offscreen.

I wave like a complete dork, and he smiles with all the love and acceptance I've come to appreciate. "Great tip, Moon. They were loading suitcases into Herman's truck when the deputies arrived."

He strides through the bullpen and holds the rickety wooden gate open for me.

"What about the kid?"

Erick's facial expression changes from satisfied to shocked in the blink of an eye. "What did you just say?"

Time for a quick subject change. "It's not important. So, Gilbert caught up with Tammy and Herman before they hit the road?"

He releases the wooden gate, and it smacks me

on the backside. My eyes open wide, and if it wasn't for the suspicious look on Erick's face, I might think he meant it in a playful way.

"You look unhappy with me, Sheriff. Did I do something?"

He drags a thumb along the side of his stubbled jaw, bites his bottom lip for a second, and shakes his head. "You and your hunches. I sent Paulsen out to the Pettit place. Gilbert's a good deputy, and he can handle riding shotgun on something like that, but I didn't think he was ready to play lone wolf."

My face nods in agreement on the outside, but my brain is spinning wildly. I know the other shoe is going to drop, and I don't want to be an ant on the sidewalk when it does. "Good call. So, she got 'em?"

He nods and gestures for me to lead the way to his office. Once inside, he lowers his voice and narrows his gaze. "When Paulsen was loading Mrs. Smythe-Wiggins into the backseat, Herman shouted something about being careful with the pregnant lady. I'm going to see what additional information I can gather during the interview, but it sounds like you already knew about the child. Mind telling me how?"

My dry throat squeaks audibly as I struggle to come up with a plausible answer.

Erick exhales and places his hand on the doorjamb. "Never mind. I'm not in the mood for a song and dance."

He steps across the hall, and my voice is barely a whisper as I call out, "Wait. Erick, I—"

"Relationships are built on trust, Mitzy." He grips the handle of the door to the interrogation room and glances back at me with more than hurt in his eyes. "You trusted me enough to tell me about your grandmother. Why are you still holding back?"

Without giving me a chance to respond, he opens the door and steps inside.

A good girlfriend would burst into the interrogation room and shout her secret to the world, but I'm just an orphan who tripped and fell into a series of fortunate events. The idea of my psychic secret being "out there" makes my chest constrict. Memories of schoolyard taunts and crying myself to sleep still have a powerful effect on my "trust" gene. Maybe I'm not a good girlfriend. Maybe someone like me is better off alone.

Shoving the emotions down where I hide all of my deepest feelings, I step into the observation room and flick the silver toggle. It doesn't take clairvoyance to see that Erick won't be taking any guff during this interview.

Tammy is nothing like I pictured her. Her sleek black hair is shinier than a raven's feather, and her eyebrows are on fleek, if that's still a thing. She's definitely watched more than one Kardashian contouring video, and if her lips are naturally that plump, I'll eat my beanie.

Erick finishes verifying names and addresses, and before he can ask any questions, Tammy launches into her performance. Don't get me wrong, it's very good, but I have certain extrasensory advantages.

She wrings her hands and weeps openly. "Sheriff Harper, you have to believe me. Oscar is a monster. He's been planning to murder Quade ever since they signed that contract. Oscar used to be a lawyer in the big city. He's cutthroat. When he had his existential crisis and quit his job, we were basically ruined financially."

Erick crosses his arms and leans back. He's clearly not going to interrupt her with any of his prepared questions. There could be some value in this one-woman show.

Herman pats her gently on the back, and she allows herself an aching sob before she continues. "When he told me he wanted to make cheese, I thought, okay, I can do it. Seeing all these online influencers making their farmstead goods, I thought I could contribute some side income with, you know, products that would support him while he figured out his business." She snuffles and draws a ragged breath. "Since we moved up here, he lost his mind. He had all these big plans for the dairy, but Quade wasn't on board. Nothing was going his way, and he started taking it out on me." She pats her chest and gasps for air.

Erick allows himself a brief question. "And that's when the abuse started?"

She nods and shudders. "Well, my men's grooming products were flying off the shelves. I had thousands of likes for my store and over 300,000 social media followers on three different platforms. I was pretty much an influencer. And he hated me for it."

Hashtag humblebrag. This Tammy is a piece of work.

Herman twists the curve of his mustache and mumbles something encouraging.

She sniffles and continues. "So, I ran into Herman at a local craft fair." She looks at him and gushes about his stache. "When I saw that mustache, it was a disaster! I just knew my special wax could help him. He started out as a customer. It was totally innocent."

My mind immediately flashes to Jessica Rabbit: "I'm not bad, I'm just drawn that way." Oh, Tammy, never responsible for your own actions, eh?

Once again, Erick speaks as little as possible. "And then the affair started?"

She looks down, in what I'm calling feigned

shame. "Yes. I'm not proud of it, Sheriff. I was in a terrible situation. Herman understood. He comforted me."

The statement catches me off guard and I snort a little as an audible response rockets from my mouth. "Is that what the kids are calling it?"

She digs through her bag for a tissue, and Erick seizes the moment. "And how long after the affair started did you ask Herman to kill your husband?"

Tammy gasps and nearly drops her tissue.

Herman leans back and shakes his head repeatedly. "Kill her husband? We never talked about killing her husband."

Erick leans toward Herman and a chill wraps itself around his next sentence. "So, who did you discuss killing?"

Tammy attempts to hide her face behind the tissue, but her eyes give her away. Something in Erick's question touched a nerve.

She dabs at her eyes, even though her airbrushed makeup hasn't budged. "Sheriff, if you're trying to figure out who murdered Quade Knudsen, you may as well know it was my husband. He had motive, means, and opportunity."

This little social media influencer has streamed one too many episodes of *NCIS*.

"That will be for the department to decide. Where were you between 11:30 p.m. and 12:30

a.m. on the night Quade Knudsen was murdered?"

She opens her mouth and gasps. "Me? What makes you think I had anything to do with it?"

For those of you at home, please note she didn't answer the question.

Erick exhales and taps his hand on the table. "Please answer the question."

"I was at home. Probably asleep. I've been having terrible nausea."

Nice one. Play the sympathy card for the poor little pregnant woman.

"Can anyone confirm that?"

She shakes her head. "Of course not, Sheriff. My husband wasn't home. He's the one that needs an alibi, not me."

"I'll let Mr. Wiggins speak for himself. How about you, Mr. Pettit? Where were you on the night in question?"

Herman pulls out his phone and scrolls through what I'm assuming is some sort of appointment app. "That was the day I had a meeting with the grocery store rep in Chicago. I took a late flight home. I was probably on the plane. Maybe I was driving home. I didn't know I would need an alibi, Sheriff. I didn't take notes on my own whereabouts."

Erick makes several of his own notes in his pad before responding. "No problem, Mr. Pettit. We can easily verify the meeting, the flight, etcetera. I'll need the name of the man you were meeting with."

Mr. Pettit twists one handlebar of his red mustache. "Of course. Hold on." He swipes and scrolls on his phone and provides the sheriff with the information.

Erick returns to questioning Tammy. "What gives you the idea that your husband killed Mr. Knudsen? Did he ever discuss plans to do so?"

Tammy shakes her head. "Not in so many words. After all, Oscar was a lawyer. He knows better than to say something like that out loud. But he always talked about how much he hated Quade, and what he would do if he owned the dairy by himself."

"If your husband had such knowledge of the law, what did he plan to do with his 49% of ownership after taking Mr. Knudsen out of the picture? Quade's will specifically listed his son as the beneficiary of his 51% share in *Udderly Brilliant*."

The moment of complete mortification that flashes across Tammy's face is definitely viral-video-worthy. She quickly schools her features and attempts to recover. "I have no idea, Sheriff. I'm sure he had some plan to outsmart the minor and move forward with whatever bigger and better plans he kept talking about. You'll have to ask him."

Erick stands, snaps his notebook closed, and

opens the door. "I intend to. We'll have additional questions for both of you after I speak to Mr. Wiggins. Deputy Paulsen will hold your passports, and we'd appreciate it if neither of you attempt to leave town while this investigation is ongoing."

A flare of anger shoots from Tammy's eyes as Herman gently pats her on the back and presses her toward the door. "I'll see that she gets home safely, Sheriff. We— We, um— We weren't planning on leaving town. She was upset. I was going to take her to the doctor."

Oh brother. Does he really think anyone's buying that? Erick doesn't even bother to reward the flimsy excuse with acknowledgment. "I'm sure we'll be chatting again real soon."

CHAPTER 20

SITTING IN THE OBSERVATION ROOM after the interview with Tammy and Herman ends, I stare at the door handle, hoping to force Erick's entrance with my mind power.

No joy.

He's upset with me, and clearly he'd rather avoid me than have an argument. I get it. There are plenty of conversations I enjoy avoiding.

Normally I'd run to Grams for advice, but something tells me this is a job for Odell.

Zipping my coat up to protect my neck and pulling my winter stocking cap down over my ears, I exit the observation room and hobble past Erick's closed office door.

I can't be sure whether the temperature has actually dropped, or if it's the chilly ache in my heart biological grandfather, I have less justification for my grandmother giving up on their relationship and marrying Cal. I always used to say that if she hadn't married Cal and had my father, I wouldn't be here. However, I've since learned that Odell is actually Jacob's father, and I'd be here whether or not she married Cal. But I still believe that everything happens for a reason. If my father hadn't been raised by a multi-millionaire railroad tycoon, he never would've rebelled. Which means he probably wouldn't have been involved in the largest armed robbery in almost-Canada. And—taking this little mental gymnastics exercise further—he wouldn't have learned the lessons he learned in Clearwater and he wouldn't have started the restorative justice program. And now my mind movies are turning into TED talks for one! "I mean, in the final analysis, everything happens for a reason, right, Gramps? The issue I'm struggling with is whether I want those things to happen right now—or not."

Odell sighs and places his weathered hand on top of my tapping fingers. "Everyone will try to tell you what to do, Mitzy. At the end of the day, you're the only one who can make the decision. You're the one who has to live with the consequences. What I think of Erick Harper doesn't matter."

Blinking back tears, I nod in agreement. "Yeah, it's the consequences that are tripping me up. Despite my—abilities—I can't seem to get a single message about those sneaky consequences."

My loving grandfather squeezes my hand. "Life isn't about knowing every outcome. Sometimes you have to take a risk. You seem like the type of girl who's more than willing to leap before she looks. What's really holding you back?" He raps his knuckles twice on the Formica countertop and returns to the grill without a backward glance.

That's an excellent question. One I don't have an answer to. For now, I'll shove it all to the back of my brain and focus on this case.

Tammy seemed hell-bent on incriminating Oscar. If she is carrying Herman Pettit's child, the desire to get rid of her current husband makes some weird kind of sense. However, a lone pregnant woman couldn't move an unconscious body from the dairy all the way out to that icehouse by herself. If Herman Pettit is the man who helped her, why was Oscar trying to hide the evidence of the dead cow at the dairy?

My stomach sours, and I shockingly exit the diner without eating anything. The more clues I uncover, the more suspects I have.

And questions! Nothing but questions.

I need to get back out to that dairy. Maybe I can figure out how the noxious gas got into the Classy

Gals' suite. There has to be something that will help narrow down the list of suspects.

I could call Quince to drive me out to the dairy, but I haven't taken any pain medication in roughly twenty-four hours, Oscar Wiggins is still in a holding cell at the sheriff's station, and I may need to get super psychic to dig up some new information.

It's probably best for everyone if I go alone.

On the drive out to *Udderly Brilliant*, I struggle with the ever-shifting facts of this case.

Quade lost consciousness because of exposure to chlorine gas, then someone moved his unconscious body out to the icehouse where they took the time to build a fire to keep him warm, but then stuffed a rag down the stovepipe to allow carbon monoxide to build up inside this tiny structure.

According to the medical examiner, he died of carbon monoxide poisoning and his body was subsequently frozen.

Did the killer predict the unseasonal temperature drop? Was it a complete shock to everyone? If so, the freezing of the corpse was never part of the plan.

But as soon as I take that off the table, I have to address the empty bourbon bottle.

I never met the victim, and I have no way of knowing whether or not he avoided alcohol due to his medication. However, Quince has a sharp eye for details and a nose for news. If he says his uncle didn't drink, I'm inclined to believe him. Which means someone poured some bourbon down an unconscious man's throat, and took an empty bottle along with the body out to the icehouse.

Why? Why would they care whether—?

Now we're straight back to the weather. If they knew about the unusual plummeting subzero temperatures, the bottle of bourbon would certainly have sent law enforcement down the wrong path.

Erick said the freeze covered any visual evidence of the carbon monoxide poisoning, and if Quince and I hadn't discovered that screw, it seems pretty likely that Quade's death would've been permanently written off as an accident.

Somebody tried to cover something up, but then they also murdered a man. Granted, they nearly got away with it, but the move to the icehouse was more than a hasty cover-up. It was an active homicide.

As I pull into the dairy, I'm shocked to see several people working in the vast barn. Truth be told, it never occurred to me that Quade and Oscar would need employees. But let's be honest, if you have five hundred cows, it's pretty unlikely that you'll be able to milk them twice a day all by yourself.

Hopefully, these employees won't give me any trouble.

Hopping out of the Jeep, I grab my crutch from the backseat and attempt a nonchalant shamble to the small milking room behind the cleanup area.

No one pays me any mind.

If I'm honest with myself, back in the days when I was working as a barista, I wouldn't have given two hoots if some stranger wandered into our stockroom. "Above my pay grade" was my standard refrain.

A quick scan of the back room reveals the open chemicals have been resealed and everything is in shipshape on this side of the suite.

Passing through the door, I take a moment to focus my energy and unleash all of my special abilities. Nothing is out of place. The collection tank stands empty, and the smell of bleach and other chemicals is thick in the air. So, it's also been cleaned.

The thing is, the cows don't come in this way— through the chemical storage area. So there has to be another exit.

Stepping around the small milking stalls, I hop a railing, pull my crutch between the bars, and walk down the ramp to a rear exit. It's a tight turn and a small ramp. All in all, the total space isn't much bigger than an average bedroom.

The rear exit has a large vented panel in the door, but someone has taped it over with plastic and duct tape. Could be a winterizing measure, or it could be a "let the chlorine gas build up inside here" measure.

Balancing myself on the crutch, I kneel to get a closer look at the plastic covering. There's a slit in the thick-mil sheet that could allow access to a tube. If someone had mixed the chemicals in a container and pushed a hose through this opening, they could have left the premises and let the gas do its work. Assuming their intent was to kill. Although, if their intent was to disable, they only needed to wait until Quade hit the floor, then they could have disposed of the apparatus, retrieved the body, and taken it to—

Shoot! His snowmobile was parked beside the icehouse. I'm certain they didn't move an unconscious body on a sled. But loading a snowmobile and a body into a truck means it has to be Oscar.

As I climb into the Jeep, I continue to twist my brain into a pretzel.

I'm overthinking this. Oscar disabled Quade, took him to the icehouse, and attempted to cover his tracks by planting the bourbon bottle. Then he tampered with the stove to create the perfect environment for carbon monoxide poisoning. The temperature drop was just a lucky break.

If that's what really happened, why do I feel so—

Before I can complete that sentence in my head, my fingers are already speed dialing the sheriff.

I place the call on speaker and start the engine to get a hint of heat going.

"Hey, I know you're upset with me, and trust me when I tell you I'm even more upset with myself. Let's call a truce until we solve this murder. All right?"

Whether his grunt is one of acknowledgment or agreement, I don't clarify. I push onward.

"Did you impound Herman Pettit's car?"

"Paulsen didn't feel the need. She loaded them into the cruiser, and Gilbert examined the vehicle for any additional evidence."

"What was in the trunk?"

"Why? Do you think they transported Quade's body in that vehicle?"

"No, but I don't want to say what I think."

He grumbles. "But you expect me to share my information."

"Erick, I promise I'm going to tell you exactly what I'm thinking. Just ask Deputy Gilbert what was in that trunk."

"Hold on." He places me on hold and comes back on the line less than two minutes later. "Two suitcases—which definitely blows a hole in the story about taking her to the doctor—a gas can and tube for siphoning gas. I suppose they didn't have time to fill up. Maybe they didn't have enough cash, and they thought they might need to steal gas as part of their getaway plan. I don't know."

"Erick, you've got to get your hands on that gas can. I'm almost one hundred percent certain that it never contained gas. I think that was part of the delivery system for the chlorine gas."

There's a long silence on the other end of the phone. "Hunch?"

"Not even close. This was straight up investigative work. I went back to the dairy and found a thick sheet of plastic taped over the vents on the back door of the Classy Gals' suite. There was a narrow slit that would've allowed a tube to be slipped through to deliver the chlorine."

He exhales. "Nice work, Moon. We'll take care of it."

CHAPTER 21

BACK AT AMATEUR SLEUTHING HEADQUARTERS, there's a sheriff's cruiser parked in the alley, blocking the entrance to my garage.

Uh oh.

The good news is, the lights aren't flashing, so it's safe to assume I'm not going to be accused of murder—for like the third time!

Turning off my engine, I hop—and that's literally on one leg—out of my Jeep, and grab my crutch from the backseat.

By the time I've organized myself and all my accoutrements, Erick is approaching with an uncertain but hopeful look on his face.

My eyes dart nervously. "Hey."

He offers a weak smile. "Hey."

Taking a step back, I slam the rear door and tilt

my head toward the bookshop. "Can we talk inside?"

He nods, hesitantly takes my keys, and opens the heavy metal alleyway door.

I crutch my way inside while he eases the door closed behind us.

My volunteer employee, who either purposely ignores our entrance or is so engrossed in entering the weekly order that she doesn't hear us, occupies the back room.

Shrugging, I continue toward the spiral staircase.

Erick silently rushes ahead and unhooks the chain for me.

The thirty-second timer counts down in my head, and I hurry to the best of my clumsy abilities. He secures the chain behind us.

This silent march toward the apartment is unnerving, but I can't think of anything to say. Apologizing without details seems hollow.

He pulls the candle handle, and we both stare straight ahead, like strangers in an elevator, while the bookcase door slides open.

Inside the apartment, I lean my crutch against the back of the sofa, remove my winter gear, and ease onto the seat. Before I have a chance to handle it myself, Erick scoops up my injured leg and elevates it onto the settee.

"Thanks."

He nods and lowers himself onto the scalloped-back chair.

An awkward quiet thickens the air between us, and there's a great deal of fidgeting and swallowing. Neither of us has a chance to break the silence.

"Oh, Mitzy! I'm so glad you're back." Grams bursts through the wall from the bookshop and surges toward me. She sees Erick and stops short. "Oh dear, did I interrupt?"

In an attempt to handle otherworldly protocol properly, I inform Erick first. "Grams is here."

His eyes track back and forth across the room and he shrugs. "Can she give us a minute?"

Grams presses a hand to her lips and arches one perfectly drawn eyebrow. "This looks serious, dear. Is everything all right?"

"We need some privacy, Grams. Understood?"

Her eyes widen and shimmer simultaneously. "I'll make myself scarce. But I'll expect a complete update later."

Before I give her my verbal response, I send her a brief telepathic message. *This is personal and private. Don't expect any details.* Then I offer the verbal response for all souls in the room. "Thanks. Bye for now."

Ghost-ma crosses her arms and vanishes in a huff.

Erick sighs. "All clear?"

"All clear."

He offers the first olive branch. "I got a judge to sign a warrant pretty fast. Paulsen and Johnson headed out to the Pettit farm to see if that gas can is still in the trunk. If not, the warrant allows us to search the property and impound the car if necessary."

He's volunteering information and using his business voice. Not good.

Erick leans back, folds his hands in his lap, and looks at me with irresistible puppy-dog eyes.

As irresistible as he is, I'm not ready. I thought about everything Odell said, and I thought about my life here in Pin Cherry, and I absolutely thought about how much I care for Erick. And at the end of all that thinking, I landed on not revealing my deepest secret. Odell got me thinking about what was really holding me back, and it's stupid and selfish.

To his credit, Erick sits in patient silence, while my brain continues to spin in circles.

I lost my mother at eleven, I ping-ponged through mostly hellish foster care for over six years, and then I landed in Pin Cherry Harbor.

I'm happy here. I'm special. I'm useful. One slip up, and all of that goes away. I know how it sounds, but I can't go back to the way things were before. Maybe my outlook is too doomsday, maybe it will change, but, right now, I know I'm not ready. So, I'm going to tell a little white lie, and you're going to have to trust me when I say it will all work out.

Sheriff Harper scrapes his hand across his polyester pant leg and exhales. "I don't want there to be any secrets between us, Mitzy. I may not be able to see ghosts, but I can see you're hiding something."

Before he throws down an ultimatum or a *Sophie's Choice*, I float my falsehood-filled balloon. "It's the pain meds. I was taking too many. I don't know whether it made me hallucinate or just made me super crabby, but it wasn't good. Grams actually flushed my pills down the toilet! So I'm clean and sober." I lift my hands as though it's a holdup. "Clean and sober, and ready to apologize."

His need to believe me supersedes his years of training. In a flash, he's kneeling next to the sofa, slipping his arm around me and gently touching my face. "I knew something was off. You know how much you mean to me, right?"

Emotion constricts my throat, and I simply nod.

Erick kisses me softly and smooths the hair back from my face. "Mitzy, I love you. I've never felt this way about anyone. I want—"

My lips are on his, and I have to stop him from saying whatever he's going to say next.

When I come up for air, I struggle to take control of the conversation. "Erick, I love you. I've never said that to any living soul besides my mother —and look what happened to her." I'm powerless to hold back the tears.

He scoops his arms around me and whispers into my neck. "What happened to your mother was terrible. I can't begin to imagine what you went through in foster care, but that part of your life is over. You deserve good things. Trust is a risk, but I promise it'll be worth it."

Between my sniffles and sobs, I manage to whisper, "I'm scared."

He kisses my cheek. "We're all scared. Let's be scared together. It's so much better than being scared alone."

"All right."

I'm not sure what I've agreed to, or what he actually offered, but something shifts. Whether it's in the real world or in my psychic fantasy, I can't be sure. Wherever it's occurring, it's wonderful, and my heart feels as though it can't fit inside my rib cage.

Without asking, he scoops me from the settee and carries me to my four-poster bed.

My tingly tummy gets the wrong idea.

Matters are quickly clarified as he places me on the down comforter. "You told me your mother used to read to you, and after she passed away you avoided books. Then the universe dumped a book-shop in your lap. I think the underlying message is clear."

I swipe at the tears on my cheeks. "Oh, is that so? And what do you think the underlying message is, Sheriff?"

He bends and kisses my forehead. "You're surrounded by books. Clearly, I should read to you." He grabs a pillow, gently lifts my injured leg, and elevates it. "What's the title of your choosing, Miss Moon?"

Without warning a deeply buried memory rockets to the surface like a torpedo. "*The 18th Emergency?*"

He scrunches up his face. "Are you asking me or telling me?"

"*The 18th Emergency*. That's the book my mother was reading to me . . . Well, you know what I mean."

Erick nods. "You never finished the book?"

"Never. Until this moment, upon pain of death, I couldn't have remembered the title. I buried it. I mean, like, super deep."

He smiles. "Stay put." Without waiting for a response, he exits the apartment.

I'm assuming he's headed downstairs to consult with Twiggy. The odds of such an old, random title being in my actual bookstore seem about the same as the odds of being hit by a meteor.

When he returns less than five minutes later with a book in his hands, I have to wonder if it's time to check the skies.

"You can't be serious? Is that it? Was it in my shop this whole time?"

He smiles, but there's a strange look in his eye. "It wasn't. Twiggy said this book arrived two days ago in an unmarked package."

The hairs on the back of my neck tingle, and I swear I can feel my mother in the room. "No way."

He turns the book toward me and shows me the cover. "Way."

The sight of the unmistakable red-and-white cover unlocks a series of memories. An emotional montage explodes inside my head.

My backpack.

Our little apartment.

My mother's loving gaze.

Her soft British voice reading me to sleep.

An aching whisper escapes my lips. "Mama, I miss you."

Erick lays the book on the nightstand and scoops me into his arms. "I wish I could've met Coraline. I know from the picture we found that you have her eyes. But if the eyes are the windows to the soul, I feel as though I kind of did meet her."

I cry it out in his arms. Eventually, the tidal wave of emotion subsides.

He releases me and grabs a box of tissues from the bathroom. When he hands them to me, I mop the years of shuttered pain from my face.

Without another word, Erick retrieves the book from the nightstand, drags the scalloped-back chair to the bedside, and sits. "Shall I start from the beginning?"

If I open my mouth, I'll start sobbing again, so I nod and grab another tissue.

"The pigeons flew out of the alley in one long swoop . . ."

The gentle cadence of his voice soothes my spirit and eases my pain. Without realizing it, I drift into a dreamland filled with happy memories of my mother.

CHAPTER 22

MORNING TOUCHES my heart with a flash of sadness as the Technicolor memories of my mother fade to black. I twist toward the pillow beside me, seeking comfort. Instead of a handsome sheriff, I find it cradles a single sheet of paper.

As I reach for the note, Grams slowly sparkles into existence beside the bed. A tear is trickling down her cheek as she clutches a strand of pearls. "I'm telling you right now, sweetie. If you don't marry that man, I will burn all your snarky T-shirts!"

"Easy, Beetlejuice. I'm barely awake. And it seems like you're reading my mail now, as well as my thoughts."

"It was out in the open—"

"Save the excuse-planations, Grams. Let me

read what I'm guessing is a lovely note from my boyfriend, before you threaten me or my precious tees any further."

She sniffles and floats backward a few inches.

Gripping the note in one hand, I roll onto my back and read these lovely words:

Dear Mitzy,

I know I can never fill the hole left when your mother passed, but thank you for letting me read you to sleep. Happy to do it any time. I said relationships are built on trust, and I have to admit it's a two-way street. I love you enough to spend the rest of my days earning yours. After you grab some breakfast at Myrtle's Diner, head into the station to observe my follow-up interview with Oscar Wiggins.

Yours for as long as you'll have me, Erick.

Of course, silent tears are streaming down my cheeks by the time I finish reading the note. I don't know what I did to deserve the world's best boyfriend, but I'm going to do everything in my power not to screw it up. When Silas gets back to town, I plan to bribe him into teaching me some type of transmutation for building trust. I'm sure it exists somewhere inside of me, but it's buried under so much trauma I can't seem to get a solid grip on it.

Grams has had all she can take. She swirls forward and wraps her ethereal arms around me. "He's got to be the best man on the planet, dear. And he's lucky to have you, too. I know you have to process some things, but don't take too long. A gentleman like that isn't one-in-a-million—he's once-in-a-lifetime."

I snuggle into the warm energy of acceptance that envelops me, and offer the only response I can find. "And how would you know?"

She swishes back and looks at me in shock. My poker face melts into loving laughter, and Grams shakes her head. "Oh, dear! You're referring to Odell, aren't you?"

"I am. I would have to say that he's your once-in-a-lifetime, right?"

She gazes out the six-by-six windows overlooking the still frozen great lake, presses a hand to her heart, and sighs with emotion. "He is. I only wish I'd realized it while I was still living that lifetime."

"Don't beat yourself up. We all have regrets. The wonderful news is that you and Gramps are finally getting a second chance. It's a super weird second chance, with all sorts of afterlife abnormalities, but still—"

Ghost-ma swirls toward me and attempts to grip my hand in hers. Her emotions are causing her to flicker, and it feels as though the heat of a candle flame is moving closer and farther away.

"You better go and get your breakfast, dear. Don't keep that sweet man waiting."

"Copy that." Lifting my slacker leg out of the bed, I teeter to a standing position. "Hey, my ankle feels a lot better."

Grams rockets to the crutch, pushes it toward me, and plants a fist on her silk-and-tulle-covered hip. "Don't spoil it by taking chances."

"Yes, mistress." Gingerly stepping forward to take the crutch, I slip it under my left arm and stumble into the bathroom to prepare myself for the day.

All the while, she's attempting to talk me into something with a plunging neckline, but I have to insist on my standard skinny jeans and a T-shirt. However, I play a little fast and loose with the top half of my outfit. The tee features a small stand of black-and-white birch trees and the tagline "Basic Birch."

When I reach for my puffy coat, she snatches it and floats toward the ceiling. "At least wear the red Olivia wool wrap coat. Please, dear. In honor of my missing trench." Her ghost eyes are wide and pleading.

"Seems like I don't have a choice, since you coat-napped my usual option!" I storm into the closet, grab the Olivia coat, and slip it on as I march out of the bookshop.

Once I'm clear of her thought-dropping, I admit the coat is fabulous.

Breakfast is quick and uneventful. Odell chuckles at my T-shirt and wishes me luck with the case.

When I arrive at the sheriff's station, I'm shocked to discover Furious Monkeys not on duty.

"Hey, Deputy Johnson, where's Furi— I mean, Deputy Baird?"

He smiles and shrugs. "Everybody gets a little time off once a week."

"Good policy." I point to the sheriff's office. "Is it all right if I head back?"

He grins too easily. "I'm not going to be the one to say no to the sheriff's girlfriend."

I roll my eyes entirely for his benefit and head back to Erick's office. As I approach the doorway, he's bent over some paperwork on his desk, which has him so engrossed, he doesn't hear me.

My extra senses float the word *party* to my brain, and I attempt to shuffle backward before I publicly spoil the surprise that I already secretly know about.

Depending on how well you know me, you may have figured out what happens next. I catch the walking boot encasing my sprained left ankle on the tip of the crutch and fall backward.

The commotion brings the sheriff running out of his office. He takes one look at me and shakes his head. "I'm not even going to ask what happened. I'm simply going to help you back on your feet, Moon."

"Thank you kindly, Sheriff Harper."

He chuckles, grabs my crutch in one hand, and lifts me to my feet with the other. "Are you okay? You didn't break or sprain anything else, did you?"

A silly grin curves up the corners of my mouth, and I give my backside a little slap. "Right as rain. It's almost like the powers that be knew I needed some extra padding back here."

He kisses my cheek softly and whispers for my ears only, "Did you sleep all right?"

My tummy flip flops and my skin tingles where his breath brushed across it. "I did. When I woke up, I found a deliciously sweet note in my bed from an amazing man."

Erick leans back, and his eyes widen. "Some man left a note in your bed? Is it a stalker? Should I send deputies over to dust the scene for prints?" He chuckles before he can finish the ruse.

"Ha ha. You're welcome to send deputies over anytime you want. The only prints they're going to find are yours!" I flash my eyebrows and whisper, "And they're everywhere!"

Now it's his turn to blush with embarrassment. He quickly changes the subject. "Let me get you set up in the observation room, and then I'll grab Wiggins from the cells."

As he turns to lead the way, I grip his hand and mumble, "Thanks for trusting me. I'm sorry I need more time."

He squeezes my fingers. "Take all the time you need. I'm not going anywhere. Are you?"

Too many emotions are bubbling too close to the surface. Time to use a little of my so-called humor to reset the vibe. "Absolutely. I'm *going* into this observation room. Sound good?"

His shoulders shake with laughter as he leads the way, and fetches an extra chair to elevate my leg.

I may not be a bonbon-eating heiress, but I can't say I mind being tended to by the world's sweetest man.

CHAPTER 23

ERICK LEAVES me to my own devices, and a few moments later he leads Oscar Wiggins into Interrogation Room 2.

Wiggins is much the worse for wear. His super-groomed facial hair is wild. Stubble covers the entire lower half of his face, and I'd swear his beard is growing faster than a werewolf's hair in the full moon. Just guessing.

The sheriff presses the record button, reminds Oscar of his Miranda rights, confirms he wants to proceed without counsel, and launches directly into the tough questions.

"Mr. Wiggins, additional evidence has come to light that puts you squarely in the crosshairs of a homicide charge. Right now, the district attorney is looking at murder one. Too many components of this crime were premeditated, as evidence will support. Your wife already shot a hole in your alibi. She claims you were not home on the night in question, and she indicates you had motive, means, and opportunity."

Now I know Erick is bluffing. He would never say something like that to a suspect. But he only has disconnected bits of evidence, and he needs a confession to seal the deal.

Reaching out with all of my senses, the regulars and the extras, I wait for Oscar Wiggins to reply.

"What? I'm not the one who killed him! I found him collapsed in the small milking room and I dragged him out of there around 10:00 p.m."

Erick nods. "If that's true, why didn't you call for medical assistance?"

"Well, there was a half-empty bottle of bourbon right inside the door, and I knew Quade wasn't supposed to mix alcohol with his medication. He always had soda water when he came to our house for supper. I figured something awful must've happened. Bad news, you know? Something about the ex-wife and the son . . . I had no idea. But I knew that negotiations with the big dairy down south were tenuous at best. I couldn't afford for him to wake up in that state and take it as a bad omen."

Erick folds a few pages over in his notebook,

taps his pen on a specific page, and continues. "So you claim you found the body, and then what?"

There's a sensation that Oscar is struggling with the next part, but I'm not able to get a clear read on why.

"I moved the body."

Sheriff Harper writes something in his notepad. "So you're the one who moved Quade's unconscious body to the icehouse where he froze to death?"

Why would Erick say that? The ME's report stated carbon monoxide poisoning as the cause of death.

Oscar leans forward and wrings his hands. "Look, I'm a lawyer, Sheriff. You're trying to get me to confess because you don't have a solid case. I'm here to tell you I didn't kill him. I loaded his sled in the back of my truck, put him in the front, and grabbed the bourbon bottle for set dressing. Then I took him to his icehouse, poured a little bourbon on his shirt, and left the empty bottle next to his chair." Oscar lifts his hands in a plea for understanding.

"Unfortunately, Mr. Knudsen's lifeless body was discovered in that very icehouse. You've admitted you placed the body. Why should I believe you aren't responsible for his death?"

Oscar shakes his head in disbelief. "Because I built a huge fire in his stove. I put in birch bark,

260 / TRIXIE SILVERTALE

some of the newspaper he had there, and several logs. Figured he'd sleep it off, wake up and not really remember what happened. I thought if he woke up in the icehouse, that would remove any suspicion about the dairy deal."

"Why would he be suspicious about things at the dairy?"

In Oscar's haste to clear his name, he may have said too much.

"Okay. Okay. To be perfectly honest, Quade wasn't entirely on board with the deal with the big dairy."

Clapping my hands together with satisfaction, I mumble, "I knew it."

"Tammy was sick and tired of being a farmer's wife. I was coming home every day smelling of cow manure and Lord knows what. She'd had enough. The deal wasn't to be sub-producers for the dairy down south. I wanted to sell the whole operation. Quade wasn't entirely convinced."

Something about Oscar's posture and the nearly imperceptible beads of sweat at his hairline tell me he's holding something back. Just as I'm about to tap on the one-way glass with the tip of my crutch, Erick swoops in. "Oscar, when you say he wasn't 'entirely' convinced, what does that really mean?"

Oscar drops his face into both of his hands,

moans, and rubs fiercely at his stubble. "I'm trying to be a good husband, Sheriff. Tammy said if I didn't close the sale, she was going to take matters into her own hands."

My eyes widen. Whoa! Here I was thinking Tammy was a behind-the-scenes Siren whispering into the ears of Oscar or Herman. Turns out she might've been the mastermind!

Erick handles his surprise with more finesse. "Mr. Wiggins, is it your statement that your wife killed Quade Knudsen?"

"No— Well, I don't know. It was such a strange coincidence. We had that big fight in the morning, and then—"

"Who had a fight? You and Quade, or you and your wife?"

"Me and the old ball and chain."

The sheriff lets all this new information simmer as he pages through his notepad. I've known him long enough and seen him conduct enough inter-views to know that the notepad is a prop. The man's mind is like a steel trap.

And suddenly, Erick takes a page from my book and tosses a question from left field. "What do you know about the gas can and rubber tubing, Mr. Wiggins?"

Oscar's messy goatee drops and his mouth hangs open like an abandoned mine shaft.

"Mr. Wiggins?"

There's a strange glint in Oscar's eye. "Was this tubing clear?"

Erick leans back and crosses his arms. "It was. How would you know that?"

Mr. Wiggins leans forward, and the expression on his face reeks of desperation. "Did you hear what I told your partner about Tammy's business? About her mad scientist stuff?"

"Are you referring to our consultant, Miss Moon?"

"Yeah, that's the one."

"Does that information have a bearing on this case?"

Oscar slams his meaty fist on the table. "Absolutely. Tammy has a pile of tubing like that. She extracts essences. I don't know. I'm just telling you, I've seen the tubing at our house. She uses that stuff all the time."

Erick uncrosses his arms, and I wish I could see his expression. His energy is tinged with anticipation. "Mr. Wiggins, you're admitting that part of the apparatus used in Quade's attempted murder comes from your house. How do you think that's going to look to the district attorney?"

"I know exactly how it's going to look, Sheriff. And you have to ask yourself if a seasoned attorney would hand you a piece of information like that—knowing full well it puts another nail in his coffin."

My head nods of its own accord. Oscar is right. If he were as talented an attorney as his wife claims, he would never be careless enough to hand the prosecution evidence.

Wiggins is nodding. "Plus, I told you, I built a fire to keep Quade warm. I didn't have anything to do with him passing out and freezing to death."

Erick leans forward and taps a finger slowly on the table as he enlightens Mr. Wiggins. "Quade Knudsen died of carbon monoxide poisoning—before his body was frozen—and with no alcohol in his bloodstream."

Oscar's eyes widen, and he leans back as this new piece of information slaps him across the face. "I opened the window."

The sheriff shakes his head. "The window was closed and locked when we discovered the body. It's your word against crime-scene evidence. Mr. Wiggins, I'm placing you under arrest—"

"Wait. Sheriff, it doesn't make sense. Even if the window was closed, the stovepipe is four inches in diameter, there's no way—"

Before Oscar Wiggins can finish that sentence, I'm rapping my crutch madly on the window.

Erick's shoulders pinch with frustration, and he suspends the interrogation.

The door to the observation room opens, and he leans in. "Yes, concerned citizen."

My eyes must be sparkling, and my heart is pounding with excitement. "The rag! I don't know why I didn't think of it before. I don't know exactly how it happened, and I think Oscar Wiggins is telling the truth. It's all about that rag."

Erick's spine straightens, and he narrows his gaze. "Hunch?"

"Not exactly. When I went out to Herman Pettit's farm and talked to him about the fence-breaking incidents, he was working on one of his machines. He stood up and wiped his hands on a rag that was tucked into his pocket. A *red* rag."

Erick's expression brightens. "If we can link one of the substances on the red rag you pulled from the stovepipe to something at that popcorn farm—"

My sudden guffaw interrupts Erick's train of thought.

"What's so funny, Moon?"

"Sorry. It was something Grams said about popcorn farmers lassoing the kernels as they popped off the cob . . . I'm sorry. It's just a hilarious visual. You know how I get."

My eyes slide to his biceps as he crosses his arms. "Oh, I definitely do, Moon. I'm going to go ahead and place Oscar under arrest, in case this rag theory doesn't pan out. If I don't charge him with something, I have to let him go. And whether he's guilty or innocent, I don't think him being free is a good idea right now."

Erick returns to the interrogation room and, as he's placing Wiggins in handcuffs, the cheese-maker looks directly at the large pane of one-way glass and shouts. "Tammy stole the baby Jesus! Ask one of her gal pals on that church committee!"

Getting to my feet, I pat myself on the back and smile. "And that's what we call a *twofer*. Two crimes solved *fer* the price of one."

Erick dispatches Paulsen to bring Herman and Tammy back to the station. Excitement is high, and I have a slip of paper in my other coat with a suddenly pertinent list of names.

As I rush back to the bookshop—as fast as crutchingly possible—A quick call to Silas confirms he landed safely and will be at his brother's bedside, but reachable by phone in case of emergency. I'd love to tell him not to worry about me, but I think we all know that would be futile.

Grams dropped my puffy coat on the settee when she abandoned the apartment. I can't believe I forgot about the list. Pulling the slip of paper from the pocket, I scan the scrawled list of names. I actually know one of these ladies. Tilly Sikanen, Tally's sister, who works at the bank.

Tilly answers on the first ring. "First Bank of Pin Cherry, how can I invest in your day?"

"Hi, Tilly. It's Mitzy Moon. I'm in a hurry so I'll get right to it. Tammy Smythe-Wiggins stole the baby Jesus and I'm trying to figure out where she put it."

"Oh, my goodness! I supported a fix up of the set, but not vandalism. Good gracious! Was anyone injured?"

I don't have time for folksy banter. "We'll discuss it later. Any idea where she might've stashed the Messiah?"

Silence. Well, not complete silence. There's a soft humming.

"Any clue would help."

"You know, I think I saw her at Second Chance Finery a few days ago. They have the cutest—"

"Thanks, I'll check it out." I hate to be rude to any of the Sikanens. They are one of the nicest families in all of Pin Cherry . . . But the clock is ticking.

Second Chance Finery is a historic home converted into a functional storefront for the First Methodist Church's fundraising and outreach ministry. The thrift shop spans the first and second floors, and the basement houses a soup kitchen. If that statue of the infant Savior is here—it definitely qualifies as irony.

The elderly ladies organizing donations and

pricing items are too absorbed in their gossip to take notice of me.

Perfect.

Reaching out with my extra senses, I feel for the Nativity statue.

A gentle warmth creeps up my left side. As I turn toward the sensation and walk along the racks, the heat increases.

At the end of the aisle, the temperature reaches unbearable levels and I'm forced to unzip my coat.

My whole body vibrates like a bed in a cheap motel. Not that I have first-hand knowledge, but I've seen the movies.

My left hand moves as though a rope is pulling it.

My fingers grip a coat on the rack.

I expect to slide the coat to the side and reveal the hidden baby—

Nope.

The COAT!

I may not have found the child of God, but I found Isadora's baby!

The Vivienne Westwood Worlds End Black "Witches" Trench Coat is in my grasp.

There's no baby Jesus at this thrift store, but the lead paid off. I overpay for the coat and drive straight back to the bookshop—at a reasonable speed on the icy winter roads.

Abandoning my crutch at the bottom of the wrought-iron spiral staircase, I hobble-step to the apartment, shouting shamelessly all the way. "Grams! Grams! I found it!"

Her face pops through the sliding bookcase like a creepy attraction at an amusement park haunted house, and the shock nearly knocks me off balance.

"You found what? The missing Nativity statue?"

Lifting the coat toward her as though it were a sacred offering, I take a clumsy bow. "The coat!"

Her image flickers, and a moment later, oodles of ghost tears spill from her eyes. "Oh, Mitzy!" She attempts to take the jacket from my arms, but her emotions are running high and sapping her energy.

I head into the apartment, and carefully arrange the precious garment on the settee for her viewing. "Now, I expect the full story. I can't explain what forces conspired to bring me and this blasted coat together, but I deserve to know why it's so important."

She floats toward the coat and reaches through the fabric. "It's still here."

Kicking out my hip, I attempt to steady myself on my good leg. "Are you trying to tell me you left something in a coat pocket forty years ago and it's still there?"

Her ethereal fingers wrap around my hand and

pull it toward the left lapel. Pressing my fingers into the coat, I feel the object in my heart before I feel it in my hand. "It's a ring."

She nods, blubbers for a few more seconds, and then smiles as though the sun rises only for her. "It's the wedding ring Odell gave me. I told Cal I'd gotten rid of it, but I couldn't. I sewed it inside the lining of my favorite coat—right above my heart."

Now we're both crying.

"I brought your father home from the hospital in this coat. I can't tell you how much it means to have it back, dear."

"I understand, Grams. I can't believe you dressed in designer duds to bring home a baby, but I'm sorry I gave you a hard time about the coat. It all makes sense now."

Her glimmering arms encircle me, and my whole body hums with love.

"Do you want me to get the ring out of there?"

She explodes like a firework and her joyful voice echoes through the room. "Yes, please! I'd love to see it again."

Grabbing my emergency-haircut scissors from the bathroom, I approach the coat with purpose. Grams coalesces into a nearly solid wall in front of me. "Don't you dare cut a hole in that priceless coat!"

"I'm only going to snip a few stitches. I promise

I'll be careful, and if I'm not able to fix it, I'll personally take it to the tailor in Broken Rock and see that it's done properly."

She flutters with relief and allows me to complete the task.

"Here it is." I cradle the ring in my palm and hold it up for her to view.

"It's the simplest and cheapest of all my wedding rings, but it holds the most valuable place in my heart." She surges with emotions.

I examine the plain circle of gold, with barely a flake of a diamond in the setting, and smile when I see the inscription. "To Myrtle: My forever."

She glows with love.

"Grams, I'm going to put this in your jewelry box. I'll leave the lid open so you can admire it, but I have to get back to the station. We are about to break this case wide open!"

She silently follows me to the jewelry box and floats in a bubble of happiness as I slip out of the apartment.

One day, I hope someone feels that way about me. Maybe *someone* already does. I need to put my big-girl pants on and take that leap Odell mentioned. Seems like Gramps knows more about romance than I ever will.

CHAPTER 24

Paulsen drags Herman Pettit into Interrogation Room 1, while Deputy Johnson deposits Tammy in Interrogation Room 2.

Gazing through the one-way glass at Tammy, I'm eager to watch Erick pry the truth from her lying, over-plumped lips. However, my head whip pans to the other side when he enters Room 1 first and sits down to question Herman.

"Mr. Pettit, I'm sure you understand how things work in a situation like this. When there's more than one person involved in the conspiracy to commit murder, the person who cooperates always gets a better deal."

Herman Pettit twists manically at his red handlebar mustache. The gesture would be hilarious if the situation weren't so grim.

Erick waits patiently, allowing the information to sink in and hopefully motivate Mr. Pettit.

Nothing is happening, and I skipped the line for patience. The delay is driving me nuts. Maybe I should tap on the window and offer to come and tell Herman about the rag I saw tucked in his pocket. Before I make my move, Erick bluffs with the confidence of a seasoned poker player.

He places an evidence bag containing the soiled red rag pulled from the stovepipe on the table and lets it sit like a grenade between them.

The panicked waves of fear rolling off Herman Pettit tell me everything I need to know. Each time I see Erick in action, my respect for his instincts grows. I have the benefit of my psychic abilities to predict that Herman is about to crack, while the sheriff is simply using his years of experience and going with his gut.

Herman twists his mustache so viciously, it tugs at the corner of his mouth.

Erick takes a deep breath and pulls the proverbial pin from the evidence grenade. "You are aware that we obtained a warrant to search your property, Mr. Pettit. Would it surprise you to know that we discovered several rags exactly like this one?"

Herman shakes visibly, leans back in his chair, and the hand that was twisting the mustache slowly creeps across his mouth as though he's keeping a terrible secret. Which, to be fair, he is.

The sheriff moves in for the kill. "This evidence bag holds the rag we pulled from the stovepipe at Quade Knudsen's icehouse. The medical examiner's report confirms that he died of carbon monoxide poisoning. Whoever put this rag into that stovepipe is looking at a first-degree murder charge. That's life in prison, Mr. Pettit. Is there anything you'd like to tell me before I go and offer Tammy the same deal?"

And the tower of Jenga blocks falls!

"Listen, Sheriff, you gotta understand. She was in a horrible situation. She's carrying my child. I had to do something."

"She can file for divorce. Things could've been handled in court. The thing that doesn't check out, Mr. Pettit, is why would you go to the trouble of creating a dangerous substance like chlorine gas and then—"

Herman doesn't allow the sheriff to finish the hypothetical. He's eager to spill the beans. Pyewacket's omniscience is irrefutable.

"It wasn't my idea, Sheriff. I was cleaning up her mess."

Erick's shoulders relax, and a confession is imminent. "Cleaning up whose mess?"

Herman gives his mustache a final tug before he grips the edge of the table and tells all.

Tammy came up with the idea to kill Quade. She devised the device to deliver the gas, and she placed the apparatus at the dairy. According to Herman, Tammy wanted to kill Quade at the dairy in order to frame Oscar. Two birds with one stone or some such logic.

When Oscar discovered his unconscious partner and moved the body out to the icehouse, Tammy had to come up with a new plan. She couldn't risk Quade regaining consciousness.

Doing his mistress's bidding, Herman drove his snowmobile across the frozen lake, closed and locked the window, stoked the fire, shoved the rag into the stovepipe, and jammed the lock with a screw to be safe.

The cold snap was a bonus they hadn't predicted, but Herman was sure the empty bottle of booze would explain how Quade passed out and let the carbon monoxide get the best of him.

"Let me make sure I understand what you're saying, Mr. Pettit. It's your statement that Tammy Smythe-Wiggins planned to murder Quade Knudsen at the dairy and frame her husband for the murder. Is that correct?"

"Yes, Sheriff. That's exactly what happened. She even figured out how to clone Quade's phone so she could text the brother. I wouldn't have even gotten involved, but—"

Erick leans forward. "But you had to clean up her mess."

He nods. "Yes. Yes. Like I said, it wasn't my idea."

"Unfortunately, Mr. Pettit, Quade Knudsen died of acute carbon monoxide poisoning, not exposure to chlorine gas, and the elements froze him postmortem. The only person who committed murder was you."

Herman's shoulders and his mustache seem to sag simultaneously. Erick doesn't deal the final blow and place him under arrest. Instead, he lets Herman Pettit stew in his own mustache wax, and steps into the hallway.

With the case wrapped up, there's only one thing left.

I may know she stole the baby Jesus from the Nativity scene, but I won't truly feel satisfied until I return the infant to the First Methodist Church.

A while ago Silas taught me a neat little trick—I mean, transmutation—for snatching an answer from someone's mind whether or not they speak it out loud. It's something to do with how people instinctively answer truthfully in their mind before they choose how to respond verbally.

I haven't been practicing this one, so I'm not

sure how it will turn out, but it can't hurt to try. Poking my head into the hallway, I see no sign of Erick.

As quick as I'm able, I pop into Interrogation Room 2 and smile as Tammy and Deputy Johnson both turn my way. "Hi, Tammy. I was hoping you could tell me where you put the baby Jesus?"

Taking a deep breath, I reach out with everything I've got in the "extra" tank. Wait for it . . . Bingo! There's the location I need! "Did you really think you could force the church into replacing the historical gifted Nativity, by stealing part of it?"

Tammy presses her lips together to stifle her reply, but she can't stop her head from nodding in agreement.

Yeesh! This woman suffers from a severe lack of imagination.

With a Cheshire-cat grin pasted across my face, I close the door and hobble into Erick's office. "I know where the baby Jesus is!"

He looks at me, scrunches up his face, and chuckles. "Would you like to share?"

"Hiding in Herman's hayloft!"

Laughter spills from the sheriff's perfect mouth. "Sounds like a tongue twister. Is it a hunch it's hiding in Herman's hayloft?"

"I deserve that." I let him have his moment, before waving it away with a flick of my wrist. "Can somebody take me out there to recover it?"

He smiles, gets to his feet, and pulls Deputy Johnson into the hallway. "I need you to take Miss Moon out to the Pettit farm. Our existing warrant covers the barn."

Deputy Johnson looks from Erick to me, and back again. "10-4, Sheriff."

On the drive out, Johnson twists his hand back-and-forth around the steering wheel as though he's trying to peel an onion layer by layer.

"What's on your mind, Johnson?"

"Um, Tammy didn't answer you. I was in the room and she didn't say anything. So, how do you know it's at the farm?"

Oops. Plot hole. When in doubt, lie it out. "I don't know anything for certain. It's sort of a hunch."

A strange smile creeps across his face as he nods. "My dad says the angels talk to you. Is that true?"

I'd only heard one person in town spouting this crazy theory. "You're the preacher's kid?"

Deputy Johnson laughs so hard tears leak from the corners of his eyes. "10-4. I haven't heard that since high school."

"Hmmm. The pastor of the First Methodist Church is your dad. Are you a typical preacher's kid? Did you get into law enforcement to make up for your misspent youth?"

Johnson's face turns serious, and he tilts his head toward me. "Wow. He was right about you. You really do know stuff."

I hate to burst Deputy Johnson's bubble and tell him that tropes about preacher's kids exist because they're often true, and that there was no angelic chorus whispering in my ear. However, I prefer to stay focused on the mission at hand before we get sidetracked. "Honestly, let's not give me too much credit. I'd rather focus on getting that Nativity scene back together."

He nods. "10-4."

At the Pettit farm, Deputy Johnson scrambles up the ladder into the hayloft and dust rises as he tosses bales, and sifts through loose hay. "I found Him!"

From the ground floor, I can't resist. "Are you saying you found Jesus, Deputy Johnson?"

He hurries to the edge of the hayloft and holds the infant Savior aloft as though he's reenacting a scene from *The Lion King*. "I found—"

My laughter floats up, and he shakes his head. "Oh, I hear it now."

"I figured you would, Deputy. Bring Him on down. I'll let you be the one to call your father and give him the good news."

Johnson tucks the baby Jesus under one arm like an oversized football and climbs down the ladder. "My dad's not too worried about it. I'm going to call Mrs. Coleman. She said she hasn't slept a wink since the theft corrupted the historical scene."

"You're a good egg, Johnson. Pin Cherry Harbor is lucky to have you."

His phone is in one hand as he waits for Mrs. Coleman to answer. He looks at me and smiles wistfully. "Nah. I'm not taking any credit for this. It's you that we're lucky to have."

And while he breaks the good news to Mrs. Coleman, his words sink into my heart. Maybe the town is lucky. Maybe I'm lucky.

Either way, if home is where the heart is, Pin Cherry Harbor is home.

End of Book 17

A NOTE FROM TRIXIE

Say *cheese*! Pyewacket continues to be my hero! I'll keep writing them if you keep reading . . .

The best part of "living" in Pin Cherry Harbor continues to be feedback from my early readers. Thank you to my alpha readers/cheerleaders, Angel and Michael. HUGE thanks to my fantastic beta readers who continue to give me extremely useful and honest feedback: Veronica McIntyre and Nadine Peterse-Vrijhof. And big "small town" hugs to the world's best ARC Team – Trixie's Mystery ARC Detectives!

My fantastic editor Philip Newey definitely saved my bacon on this one. Thanks to him, I satisfyingly filled a major plot hole. I'd also like to give a heaping helping of gratitude to Brooke for her tireless proofreading! (Despite her holiday schedule.) Any remaining errors are my own.

I'm especially grateful for the helpful chemistry info provided by Michael. Thanks to Josh and Morgan for the mustache inspiration!

FUN FACT: When I was in the eighth grade, I had a massive crush on the son of a local dairy farmer. Cheers to what *curd* have been, Leonard.

My favorite line from this case: "Are you saying you found Jesus, Deputy Johnson?" ~Mitzy

I'm currently writing book eighteen in the Mitzy Moon Mysteries series, and I'm planning a big surprise. Mitzy, Grams, and Pyewacket got into plenty of trouble in book one, *Fries and Alibis*. But I'd have to say that book three, *Wings and Broken Things*, is when most readers say the series becomes unputdownable.

I hope you'll continue to hang out with us.

Trixie Silvertale (January 2022)

Mitzy Moon Mysteries No. 18

When our psychic sleuth lands in the middle of a Wonderland bank robbery, will she keep her cool or lose her head?

Mitzy Moon is determined not to spoil her surprise birthday party. She's been dodging questions and playing dumb for months, but a sassy snoop can only take so much. And distraction turns to madcap disaster when she's caught in a bank hold up by a gun-toting White Rabbit and his grinning gang.

Held hostage by the Mad Hatter and his masked cohorts, Mitzy's plan to get the bank employees out alive is percolating nicely. However, without the calm alchemist or her feisty feline, things are coming to a rapid boil. Help is on the way, but it could arrive too late...

Can Mitzy keep the armed gang from violent measures, or will her scheme collapse like a house of cards?

Heists and Poltergeists is the eighteenth book in the hilarious Mitzy Moon Mysteries paranormal cozy mystery series. If you like snarky heroines, supernatural intrigue, and a dash of romance, then you'll love Trixie Silvertale's twisty tea-party tale.

Buy *Heists and Poltergeists* to put these safecrackers in the slammer today!

Grab yours here!
readerlinks.com/l/861835

Scan this QR Code with the camera on your phone. You'll be taken right to the Mitzy Moon Mysteries series page. You can easily grab any mysteries you've missed!

Come visit Pin Cherry Harbor!

Get access to the Exclusive Mitzy Moon Mysteries character quiz – free!

Find out which character you are in Pin Cherry Harbor and see if you have what it takes to be part of Mitzy's gang.

This quiz is only available to members of the Paranormal Cozy Club, Trixie Silvertale's reader group.

Visit the link below to join the club and get access to the quiz:

Join Trixie's Club
http://trixiesilvertale.com/paranormal-cozy-club/

Once you're in the Club, you'll also be the first to receive updates from Pin Cherry Harbor and access to giveaways, new release announcements, short stories, behind-the-scenes secrets, and much more!

Scan this QR Code with the camera on your phone. You'll be taken right to the page to join the Club!

THANK YOU!

Trying out a new book is always a risk and I'm thankful that you rolled the dice with Mitzy Moon. If you loved the book, the sweetest thing you can do (*even sweeter than pin cherry pie à la mode*) is to leave a review so that other readers will take a chance on Mitzy and the gang.

Don't feel you have to write a book report. A brief comment like, "Can't wait to read the next book in this series!" will help potential readers make their choice.

★★★★★
Leave a quick review HERE
https://readerlinks.com/l/2111167
★★★★★

Thank you kindly, and I'll see you in Pin Cherry Harbor!

Heists and Poltergeists: Paranormal Cozy Mystery

Blades and Bridesmaids: Paranormal Cozy Mystery

Scones and Tombstones: Paranormal Cozy Mystery

Vandals and Yule Scandals: Paranormal Cozy Mystery

More to come!

MAGICAL RENAISSANCE FAIRE MYSTERIES

Explore the world of Coriander the Conjurer. A fortune-telling fairy with a heart of gold!

Book 1: ***All Swell That Ends Spell*** – A dubious festival. A fatal swim. Can this fortune-telling fairy herald the true killer?

Book 2: ***Fairy Wives of Windsor*** – A jolly Faire. A shocking murder. Can this furtive fairy outsmart the killer?

Join Sydney Coleman and her unruly ghosts, as they solve mysteries in a truly haunted mansion!

Book 1: ***Moonlight and Mischief*** – She's desperate for a fresh start, but is a mansion on sale too good to be true?

Book 2: ***Moonlight and Magic*** – A haunted Halloween tour seem like the perfect plan, until there's murder...

Book 3: ***Moonlight and Mayhem*** – An unwelcome visitor. A surprising past. Will her fire sale end in smoke?

ABOUT THE AUTHOR

USA TODAY Bestselling author Trixie Silvertale grew up reading an endless supply of Lilian Jackson Braun, Hardy Boys, and Nancy Drew novels. She loves the amateur sleuths in cozy mysteries and obsesses about all things paranormal. Those two passions unite in her Mitzy Moon Mysteries, and she's thrilled to write them and share them with you.

When she's not consumed by writing, she bakes to fuel her creative engine and pulls weeds in her herb garden to clear her head (*and sometimes she pulls out her hair, but mostly weeds*).

Greetings are welcome:
trixie@trixiesilvertale.com

BB bookbub.com/authors/trixie-silvertale

f facebook.com/TrixieSilvertale

O instagram.com/trixiesilvertale

Made in the USA
Las Vegas, NV
26 November 2022

60368195R00176